Marbles

An Anthology of Micro and Flash Fiction

ISBN: 978-1-962187-04-6 (Paperback edition)
ISBN: 978-1-962187-05-3 (eBook edition)

Book design by Blue Marble Storytellers.

Edited by Anna Sharples (sharpsightedgrammar.co.uk)

First printed edition 2024.
Blue Marble Publishing

Contents

5

Author Index

Introduction

During difficult times, people will always find quiet corners to write down the secrets of their hearts, unspooling their fears and attempting to understand their desires.

That's how Blue Marble Storytellers began. During the pandemic, a few like-minded wordsmiths banded together—then invited friends to come along for a marvelous journey. Since creativity begets creativity, in short order Blue Marble participants engaged in wildly innovative projects and clever collaborations, from podcasting to illustrated novels to audio recordings. New friends from around the world found Blue Marble a welcoming place that celebrated good writing.

Blue Marble's Discord channel quickly became a thoughtful place that provided guidance, camaraderie, and support to writers of all abilities. This anthology highlights short stories, flash fiction, and microfiction from some of the brightest minds on the Discord channel. Notable writers from almost every continent have submitted award-winning contest entries or pieces that are dear to their hearts.

Publisher's Note

Each story of this anthology has been faithfully reproduced as written by the author, with no attempt to standardise either spelling or grammatical style. Consequently, you will find an eclectic mix—like the stories themselves—of American and British English. This is a conscious decision on our part.

A text from you.

You want to meet me for coffee.

[Ok.]

I imagine a cozy cottage by the sea for us with a garden to sunbathe in and a view of the water. How nice it would be to have coffee there, a place so far away from here.

But I lower my expectations and add twenty pounds to your picture. I visualize your hairline much farther north. You smile, but you don't show your teeth.

Send me a video, I say.

[Ok.]

Wearing a baseball cap and a Washington Capitals hockey jersey, you appear in the digital flesh, walking your big brown dog. You flash a dazzling smile towards the camera, your eyes hidden behind dark sunglasses. I wonder who is taking the video. An old girlfriend? A current wife? I watch it like the Zapruder film.

Intrigued, I scour your social media. Your big brown dog is named Slapshot, possibly after the Washington Capitals' team mascot. Slapshot is a questionable name for a mascot and a dog, but I think of us walking your dog together, laughing, sharing our day.

I imagine a downtown New York City loft for the three of us. A short walk to restaurants, museums, theaters. A kitchen to toast bagels and slather on smoked salmon and cream cheese and capers. A view of Central Park. How nice it would be to have coffee there, a place so far away from here.

I force myself to lower my expectations. Maybe you won't like me? Sure, I am well-versed in hockey (now). I text you that I have two tickets to next week's game — a gift from a friend. This is a lie. I purchased them myself, but I cannot think about anything else other than sitting next to you in the stands, shelling peanuts, and watching grown men swing sticks and punch each other.

So, will you come to the game with me? You can explain what's happening.

[Ok.]

Your reply thrills me.

I imagine a rustic cabin in the Poconos for us, like the one my ex-husband promised me we'd build one day. A short hike to winding walking trails. A kitchen to cook up hearty vats of chili. A view of mountain ranges. How nice it would be to have coffee there, a place so far away from here.

But I am here, waiting in the coffee shop we decided on, wondering if you'll bring Slapshot since this coffee shop is dog-friendly. Instead, I look up every time the door opens, and it's everyone but you.

Each minute past the time we agreed upon is an embarrassment.

Finally, you text me that you aren't coming. You're sorry, but it's complicated. You hope I understand.

[Ok.]

But I don't understand.

I imagine our cozy cottage swallowed up by the sea, our New York City loft gutted to the studs, and our rustic cabin burned to the ground.

You wanted to meet me for coffee.

And it's [Ok.]

But I'm not [Ok.]

A Bugler's Final Note – James Lynch

(Genre: Action/Adventure)

1st of June, 1813

The mighty Chesapeake is taken! Brave and stalwart Captain Andrews lies gravely wounded in his stateroom! Our valiant crew is dying on the deck above, spurred on by their leader's final words, but they will soon be overtaken. I am afeared that blame shall fall upon me, that this thorough defeat will be placed upon my trembling lips. I hasten to write this now, even as our glorious Chesapeake is overrun by the enemy, to acquit myself of blame should I fall.

As the battle began, I stood on the quarterdeck with Captain Lawrence, my finely polished bugle held at the ready. We engaged our enemy, the Shannon of the king's navy, on the waters outside of Boston Harbor. Cannons and muskets roared between the two ships. Both ships were damaged, but the Shannon proved too strong a foe. Indeed, her gunners seemed to know every point upon which to strike. Our cannons struck the Shannon squarely but with little effect while our foe raked the Chesapeake so precisely that her topsail was rendered useless and many men fell. The Shannon's guns fired relentlessly, destroying our wheel. Musket fire buzzed through the smoked-filled air, and Captain Andrews was injured in the leg.

I saw him rise, dauntless amidst the unyielding assault. But the Chesapeake drifted, then got sternway, and the two ships became entangled. As I waited for my orders, a vile grenade flew through the air, landing in an arms chest meters from my post. I had only a breath's worth of time.

I threw myself beneath a nearby launch. The explosion tore the boards asunder, sent metal and wood like a deadly flower in all directions. It was so loud, I was certain my end was at hand.

The sounds of battle are ebbing. I fear the British will be upon me soon.

I roused myself, remarkably unharmed. But my ears, oh my ears, they rang with the sound of a thousand church bells. Smoke and flames clogged my sight. Through the miasma of war, I saw our stalwart captain waving his saber, calling out orders that my ears could not discern, so deafened I was by the explosion. I tried to rouse myself and resume my post, but my addled mind and shaking limbs refused my wishes. The British soldiers flowed like blood from their ship to ours. Captain Andrews went down again in the tumult.

He bled front and back, color draining from his face. The men carried him below. His voice, so strong and commanding, called out his final orders, overwhelming the bells in my head. "Don't give up the ship!" he cried to those around him. "Fight her till she sinks!" As the men hauled his bleeding body below, his eyes alit on mine. At that moment, my fears were birthed, for in those eyes I saw condemnation, anger, a searing, blazing gaze that branded me a coward and a failure.

The deck above me creaks and the shouts of the British approach. My time is dwindling faster than our Captain's life.

I crawled out from my shelter, my mind beginning to clear, and with the smoke to conceal me escaped to the ladders. As I made my way, I came to realize why he looked upon me with such disdain. In the tumult, he tried in vain to rally his boarders but I, with my head befuddled and my ears full of clanging bells, could not hearken to his words. Had I been able to hear, or perhaps if the other officers were not all slain by the enemy's uncompromising barrage, the tide of the battle may have turned in our favor.

I know not what fate awaits me. For the sake of my wife, who stood upon the shores of Boston Harbor with those who gathered to watch us sail into the battle that I now report upon, and that of my unborn child, I pray that this letter finds the hands of trustworthy men, and then the hands of our commanders who will surely cast judgement upon us. My final act will be to secure this note inside the only vessel I have upon me – the polished bugle that I failed to blow – with the wax and thick, soft end of a candle and cast it into the sea. I pray that history will look kindly upon me and that my name will not be uttered in the same breath as coward.

The British stomp and pound outside my door. Shall I fight them and surely die? Shall I surrender and hope for leniency? Neither end shall truly give me peace.

A Cookie for Teddy – Daniel R. Hayes

(Genre: Fantasy)

Suzie raised a chocolate chip cookie to her pink lips and took a bite. The sweet cocoa seemed to make her taste buds dance a disco cha-cha. A few crumbs fell on her blue dress, the crunchy goodness impossible to contain.

Teddy glanced at Suzie's sparkling green eyes and was happy her mind was elsewhere. He quickly stuck out his tongue for a taste. His soft cotton insides exploded like fireworks. He didn't know what this treat was, but he wanted more.

Later that night, Suzie jumped into bed and squeezed Teddy tight. He gasped for air until she let up and gave him a kiss. Sometimes she gets carried away, you see, because she loves him so much. Teddy bears are known to melt every child's heart with their velvety fur, soft button noses, and squishy insides.

The smell of pumpkin spice rocked Teddy's nostrils, but he longed for more chocolate chip crumbs. He wished Suzie would sneak out of her bedroom and grab just one. If she was quiet, her parents would never know.

Suzie's mom cracked the bedroom door to check on her beloved daughter. "Did you brush your teeth?"

"Yes, Momma."

"Good because I made a whole batch of cookies, and I don't want you to go crazy with them. They're not good for your teeth. Do you understand?"

"I do, Momma."

"Okay… just remember, stay out of the cookie jar. Good night, my angel. I love you! Have dreams as sweet as you."

"I love you too, Momma."

More cookies!!!

As the cotton raced through Teddy's mind, a plan quickly formed.

When Teddy heard Suzie's snores, he knew it was time. He pried himself free from her stranglehold and plopped to the plush carpet. He made a mad dash to the door, which was still cracked, and stumbled out. He ran down the hallway like a bouncing bunny. There was no reason to tiptoe because he was made of stuffing.

The kitchen was dark, but the red cookie jar was lit up like a beacon. *Thank goodness for the moon!*

Teddy had to figure out how to get to the cookie jar because the countertop looked like Everest. His tiny, black marble eyes grew ten times larger when he saw how high it was.

It was a good thing little Suzie took him along to her gymnastics class!

Teddy pranced backward to get some running room and did a triple somersault that sent him flying to the top of the countertop with room to spare. He was elated that he was full of stuffing.

The cookie jar was now within reach. Teddy carefully removed the lid and grabbed a sweet treat. "Oh, how I love these crunchy munchies!"

The following morning, Suzie awoke to her mother's voice. "Suzie! You forgot to put the lid back on!"

A Liturgy of Flame – Claire Lindsey

(Genre: Fantasy)

When the mages came to Edsea we set them on fire. Maether insisted they be burned on the cliff, so the spectacle might ward off any other unwanted visitors. It was a sight to behold: three bearded men in crimson robes, ablaze like torches against the dim indigo sky. The salted ocean air was choked with screams, smoke, and the scent of burning flesh. *Let the world know,* Maether's voice echoed into the night. *Let them never forget—Isle Edsea keeps the Old Ways.*

After the fires died down, Maether sent the islanders back to their homes. I stood with Adelin and the other initiates, keeping watch over the bodies until dawn. And when the sun finally crept up over the ocean and Maether returned for us, smoke still wafted from the corpses, mingling with the early morning fog.

"Itha, Adelin, tend to the mess." Maether gestured vaguely at the remains, her wide face devoid of emotion. "The rest of you will return to the temple with me for morning rites."

We nodded in practiced unison. Adelin and I watched for a moment as Maether led the line of blue-robed initiates down the steep outcrop towards the village. Above them, a pair of sea ravens flitted about along the rocky slope, searching for nests to raid for their breakfast.

"Why didn't they stop us?" Adelin asked. She inspected the bodies closely, as if expecting them to respond. Their charred jawbones hung open in eerie silence.

I had no answer. By all accounts, the mages ought to have

been capable of warding off—even obliterating—a small mob of islanders. But they had not defended themselves.

Adelin handed me a shovel, her honeyed eyes grim and cold. "Best get to work."

That evening, we trudged through the village covered in soot and soil. A small boy playing outside his doorstep saw us approach and dashed inside, calling out for his mother. Islanders bowed as we passed by their squat houses, which were designed to withstand seaborne storms. In our wake, doors were closed, children ushered away. The Old Ways did not permit them to speak to initiates.

Perched at the edge of the island atop the cape, the temple gleamed. Tall spires stretched towards the sky, unchanged by time and tide. In their shadow, I recalled a once fearful child, sent far from home to be raised in the Old Ways. A gift of obedience, to be bent and broken according to the Goddess's will.

Adelin examined her arms, her nose wrinkled in disgust. From the time I'd arrived at Edsea, she'd been my first and only friend, an orphan who'd never known a life beyond the temple and Maether's surveilling eye.

"Gods, I need a bath," Adelin said.

"You really do."

She glanced at me, mouth agape. Then she shoved me sideways with a cackle. "Ah, that's right, you always smell like you've got sea roses up your ass."

Our laughter faded as we approached the temple. The air was cooler there, in the shade of the gleaming stone. From the nearby shore, the sound of the waves rose to keep rhythm with songs and chants echoing inside. The eventide rites had already begun.

Adelin and I shuffled quickly through the side entrance and up the narrow steps to our rooms. Grabbing a pitcher, I filled a metal basin and washed the filth from my face and arms. The sight of my hands in the water, black with soot, set my heart racing. I recalled the mages' fingers: blackened, bone-thin, and so brittle that they cracked like twigs as we placed their bodies in the earth.

"Are you alright?" Adelin asked. Her face was flushed red, scoured clean of ash. Her eyes were red, too, though her expression was like stone.

I nodded, taking my time as I dried my hands so she did not see them tremble.

Satisfied that we were presentable, we crept downstairs to the sanctum.

Maether stood at the altar, beneath a window crafted from hued sea-glass. She was awash in the light of greens and blues, as if underwater. She held aloft a silver chalice and murmured an ancient incantation. Adelin and I took our places, kneeling beside the other initiates just in time to receive our blessing. Maether's voice filled the room, unwavering and constant as the tide.

"May the sea and her waves ever greet you with warmth."

I bowed my head, inhaling deeply. Ash fell from my hair, flitting like a sea raven's feather to the ground. The screams of the mages came unbidden to my mind.

"May the eyes of the Goddess turn kindly unto you."

I shivered, thinking of sunken sockets and blackened

skulls.

"May you pass like a ship on calm waters through this life."

Adelin sniffled beside me. She reached out for my hand and clenched it, weaving her fingers through mine. There was soot beneath her fingernails, crescent moons the color of pitch. I glanced up at Maether, her white gown gleaming, her pale fingers wrapped around the intricate silver cup.

Maether locked eyes with me, expressionless.

"And may your vessel be a strong one, to serve and withstand the will of the Goddess. For though she is good, she is without mercy."

I closed my eyes, letting the familiar taste of sea salt in the air clear the inferno in my mind. Adelin's hand relaxed in mine as together with the congregation, we repeated the invocation:

"For though she is good, she is without mercy."

A Worse Punishment for Murder – Michelle Oliver

(Genre: Ghost Story)

At precisely thirteen minutes past midday, Mary Green's life ended. She was quite surprised to open her eyes and see herself dangling at the end of a rope. Without her ninety-three pounds of mortal coil, she felt so much lighter as she hovered three feet above the scene.

"Hello, Mary, love. It's been a while." She'd know that voice anywhere, and thought she'd never see him again. You know the line 'until death do us part'? Well, she'd been a widow for nearly twelve months now. As the deep baritone washed over her, she could feel her non-corporeal stomach plummet.

"Jim." She turned, dread washing over her in waves. "How have you been?"

He looked as he had always done: flaccid jowls, rotund belly, beady eyes and receding hairline. However, the gaping hole in his chest was new. She tried not to look at it.

"I suppose I've been better," he shrugged, his corpulent body bobbing mid-air. "You know, like alive."

Mary stretched her neck and wriggled uncomfortably as she floated toward the ceiling.

"Ah, no you don't, Mary, love. Only the righteous ascend. I doubt you fit into that category now, do you?" He scratched his chest and she couldn't help but look. Although she could see right through him—his body was translucent—there was an open porthole in his middle. She could stick her hand right through it, but only if she dared to get that close to him. She figured silence was the only safe response.

"Been waiting a long time, Mary, love. My shirt needs ironing, and I've been waiting for you to fix my dinner."

Mary saw red. In the last twelve months, had he not once ironed a shirt, packed his lunch or cooked his own dinner? He'd probably never picked up a broom, washed a plate or wiped the counter either. Death had not changed him. Her trigger finger twitched as her lips thinned. Where was a shotgun when you needed it?

Jim scratched his armpit and lounged back on his cloud of air. "Fetch me a drink, would you, Mary, love? Been a bit thirsty and could do with a pint."

Till death do us part, Mary thought grimly. They were both dead, so it was certainly time to part. She flounce-floated away, ignoring his request for the first time in her life… or death.

Unhindered by her mortal form, she drifted through the prison walls that had been her home for the last few months. The fresh air and sunshine beckoned.

"Hey, where are you going?"

Mary gasped as Jim suddenly appeared before her. He grabbed her wrist in his icy hand and tugged. Without solid ground beneath her feet, she could not resist and tumbled against his chest. His other hand snaked around her back, pressing her close, whispering ominously in her ear.

"It's so good you're here, Mary, love. We've got eternity together, you and me."

Eternity! It was unthinkable.

Was there ever a worse punishment for murder?

All That I Am – Cristina Rose Strube

(Genre: Action/Adventure)

I have memories from long ago… so long, in fact, I think I was still inside my mother. Again and again I have been told that I shouldn't remember that far back, but I can't help it; I do.

I remember my mother trundling along clutching my siblings and me in her spindly fingers. She was looking for something - and whenever she found it, a brother or sister dropped from her grasp.

Looking back, I should have been concerned for my siblings - but I wasn't. As long as I was clutched in my mother's arms, everything was fine.

Then, at one stop, it was me slipping from her grasp.

"Mother!" I silently cried. I was sure she would realize her mistake. She would miss her child and come back for me. She never did. She ambled off into the sunset - and that was the last I ever saw of my mother.

I sat on the hot gritty sand, hoping my mother would return - yet knowing she wouldn't. When noon rolled around and the sun was too hot to bear, I burrowed myself down into the warm sand. From there my sense of time disappeared.

Years may have passed - or mere seconds - before my skull split and my head pushed up through the grime, into a bright beautiful world.

From there, I bloomed from child to adolescent. Wild animals came to nibble my fingers, devouring in seconds what I had worked long and hard to grow. The animals hurt me none; I was there to provide them food, but I hated them with an envy-born hate. I wanted to run!

When the animals came to feed, they moved with such grace - their babies frisking and frolicking nearby - while I was unable to move one small appendage without the wind's help. My leaves were green with envy.

Then the pollinators came. They took something away from me, replacing it with what they had taken from other beings of my kind. Their deposits came together with what was left of myself, blooming into perfect little children.

It was then I noticed I had left my childhood far behind. I was almost to the point Mother was when I last saw her!

The blooms withered and died, leaving my children in their hard shells, ready to be born.

I clutched my children fiercely in my thin fingers, willing to protect them as the wind battered harder and my roots grew weaker.

Finally one day a violent gust of wind tore my roots from the ground, sending me rolling across the surface of the Earth. Fear for myself and my children was fast overcome by an exhilarating realization: my roots had been holding me back! I could now roam as I pleased!

I frolicked in the hot sand until I had calmed down enough to think. As sad as it was, I knew I could not keep my children with me forever.

Sadly, I went looking for safe homes - a soft patch of sand where they could set roots and grow.

Finding the perfect spot, I let one of my babies drop

from my grasp, recalling how I'd felt as a seed. "I'm sorry I've resented you, Mother," I thought.

Now I tumble through the desert finding homes for my children, hoping they don't resent me for it. Even if they do, they will understand one day when they have children of their own.

People say I am ugly; moving free is a beautiful thing. People say I am dead; I feel more alive than I ever did rooted to the ground. I don't care what people think. I'm happy with my life… my life as a tumbleweed!

Allie – James Lynch

(Genre: Drama)

He stumbled alone through spires of black, only the light of his memory to guide him, until the trees thinned and gave way to a gentle rise where dead grass crunched beneath his feet and the stars and gibbous moon dangled diaphanous light across a clearing, and when he reached the summit of the low hill where they had spent the most perfect hours of their lives he fell to his knees, threw his arms wide, and released his grief into the frozen night. The grief geysered from his throat in a wail that shook the stillness and rattled his limbs until his bones throbbed, and when his body could finally take no more he dropped to his hands, his existence reduced to a blurry, shadowed patch of brown grass where tears landed and disappeared into crystal pools. His entire being heaved with release, breathing razors of ice that sliced his throat before melting in the churning fire of his gut. Shuddering, struggling, fragments of his agony escaping with each ragged breath. "Only needed. To see you. One last time." He remained there, prostrate and shivering, until he felt the sky shifting above him, saw his silhouette darkening beneath a growing light, and he forced his cramped spine to straighten.

Her face, translucent and perfect, filled the firmament, her gently rounded chin just above the treetops, the peak of her hair halfway up the sky. Curls of night tickled her cheeks, her silver-blue eyes full of compassion, her fiery rose lips curled into the slightest of smiles. Stars spangled her face like the mist that had enveloped them the first time they had kissed. The waxing moon, full and low, hung where an earring might have been, the tiny scar by her ear a moonlit shadow.

Her name snagged in the steamy thorns of his breath and his fingers strained to reach her. She rippled and he thought she might vanish; her lips parted just enough to see her teeth, and the corners of her eyes dimpled. He called to her again, and this time his voice freed itself from the brambles and darted across the air. "Allie?"

She wavered again, tilting alluringly to the side, silent laughter blooming on her face.

He did not question how, because he simply did not care what power had conjured this moment. The tatters of grief still clinging to his soul shriveled at the sight, the gelid air no longer a concern. "Oh my God, Allie, it's really you, isn't it? I . . . I only wanted to see you one more time. Not a picture or a memory. I wanted to see that scar where I've kissed you so many times." She rippled and turned slightly so that he could see it more clearly. "I wanted to see you, just the way you were, before . . ."

The quivering of her face made it look like she was nodding in understanding, and a subtle wink in her eye made him smile. "It's been so hard." He released the pain and sadness, letting it flow and saturate every word. "Your family refused to let me see you these last five months. I tried so hard, Allie, I even tried to go when I knew no one was there, but your family told the hospital staff not to let me in. I wanted just to see you, try to help you, to make sure you . . . you didn't blame me too."

Her face trembled, and her eyes closed for a moment, gently dismissing his fears. "Thank you," he whispered, and she smiled anew. He ignored the buzzing of his phone, focusing on her incandescent face. Words were useless; he just stared at her, immune to the winter air and time, watching the stars slowly shift behind her, the moon easing up and lighting a halo behind the dense swirls of her sable hair. He would spend this night, this last night, alone with her.

The incessant intrusion of his phone finally pulled his attention away from her heavens. He intended to turn it off, but the messages that kept appearing stopped his hand.

Dude RU seeing this?

WTF? Is that Allie?

How are you doing this? It's so cool!

He looked up again. Her smile had grown, a stray ribbon of night sky hair dangling across her forehead. He flicked on the camera and took a picture, then another. With each click the image above him dimmed. "No," he called to her, so distraught he dropped the phone, "don't go! I need you. I don't know if I can do this without you!"

Her expression changed, a look of sarcastic confidence so familiar to him it summoned fresh tears and laughter. And then she was gone from the sky, leaving only the endless universe and a smear of sunrise.

He crumpled to the ground, retrieved his phone and brought up the pictures, marred only by the stream of messages flowing across his screen. He dismissed them all until he saw a name that freed the anger caged in his heart. Jake, her brother. He swiped it open, ready to unleash it all. He saw the words, read them over and over.

He brought the images back up, staring once more into the celestial beauty of her face. Then he went back and replied to her brother.

He sent it, then dropped the phone back into his pocket. It was petty and vindictive, to keep those images to himself. But he knew she had been there for him, not for anyone else. She had chosen him, both three years prior and again this frigid night. He looked up one last time, vowing to never return to that spot, and walked back into the trees, his selfish smile keeping him warm all the way home.

Amelia's Journey Begins – Míriam Toyama

(Genre: Fantasy)

Amelia opened her bedroom door and fell. She fell because the floor wasn't where it should be. She landed on a hardwood floor. Confused, she looked up. It was a mistake; she shouldn't have. The view was terrifying. She was on what looked like a boat attached to a balloon, but it wasn't a balloon, it looked like an animal. A whale? She felt her heart skipping a beat, but mostly she felt her knees; she'd landed on them.

She tried to run to the edge of the boat. All she could see were stars, everywhere, surrounding her from all sides. She thought she could see Earth to her right. She looked up, and it was indeed a boat propelled by a whale, but whales don't fly, she thought. Immediately the boat came to a halt, and to her surprise, it started to fall, in space! A short lady in a long dress came running towards her.

"What did you do?"

"Nothing!"

"What did…? Just now! What did you believe?"

"I…whales don't fly!"

"Of course they do! Look at Suzy!"

"They live in the Ocean! They swim!" Such a weird dream! How could she breathe in space?

"Air? You're doubting air? Where the hell do you come from that you have to fight for air?"

"There shouldn't be air in space!"

"Says who?"

"Physics!"

"Wrong! Air is everywhere you need it. And Suzy, she can fly anywhere! Because you see, if we keep falling not only do we risk crashing but also I'll be late to deliver my cargo."

"It's not my fault! This place, it defies the laws of physics!"

"Oh darling, forget about this Physics person. This boy doesn't have your best interest at heart! I'm looking out for you. I don't know how things work where you came from, but here, well, here things move and work by imagination. And you've got to start believing, 'cause you are taking me way off course."

"Imagination?"

"Yes, imagine you can breathe. Imagine Suzy can fly."

"I can breathe; I can definitely breathe in space. A whale can fly in space without dying," she said, looking into the other woman's eye.

"No honey, you're making things too difficult. Stop trying to think things through, try feeling things through, OK?"

"I can breathe!" She closed her eyes, creating harsh lines on her forehead.

"Now now, feel the wind, feel the air filling you up, listen to Suzy as she moves."

"Suzy can fly!" Her eyes were still closed, tears forming in the corners, but the creases in her forehead started to disappear.

"That's it; I know it's hard at first, but just feel the Universe moving slowly and taking you with it. Feel life creeping in every corner."

Amelia felt the wind that shouldn't be there, slowly opened her eyes, and wondered how she would go home, while the tears traveled down her cheeks.

Amigurumi It Ain't – Eamon Somers

(Genre: Fantasy)

A man walks into a pub. No, a woman walks into a pub. No, a pub walks into a woman, well bumps her.

'Where do you think you're going?' she asks.

'I need a woman the way a man needs a drink,' said the pub.

'And you think that's me?' she said. 'I'm not big into pubs. I prefer to sit in front of the tele watching Murder She Wrote reruns while I crochet multicoloured doilies.'

'Are your doilies well known all over the country?' the pub asked, nudging a banquette behind her so she could sit and reminisce about *great doilies I have crocheted*.

They made a strange sight, the woman on the banquette near the bus stop, and the pub resting on its laurels on the grass verge between the bus stop and the slope down to the river, its trailing pipes peeping out from its underside and the sound of raised voices coming from within.

'No,' the woman said. She clearly wanted to change the subject, although the pub was smiling and there was no need for her to feel embarrassed, or to fear that the pub would tell the world about her shame at not achieving fame, having dedicated most of her life to doily crocheting.

'Are you a crotchety crocheter?' the pub asked, trying to loosen her up. He was a man's pub and had noticed that when men are crochety they either get into a fight or they take the piss out of each other, often to a point of humiliation. The end result is usually better than when they fight, although banter can also end in fisticuffs. 'And what about Amigurumi?'

'Once, but I'm very happy with doilies,' the woman said, doubting that she was genuinely talking to a pub, but if she was, was there any harm in it? She hadn't come across this kind of exchange before, neither in her personal life, which in fairness was reasonably limited, nor in any of the magazines she read. 'The magazines I take' – putting it this way made her feel more assertive – 'I take two magazines a week, every week.' Taking was somehow more transgressive than claiming to just read.

The pub had little time for magazines. The brewery had a couple of trade journals pushed through the door regularly, but the licensee only ever glanced at the headlines before binning them. There had been a change of reading material during the two-year period when the pub had welcomed LGBTQ+ers. Publications that it must be said upset some of the old habitues because of the pictures, but most of them came back after the brewery put a stop to them, and the queer crowd moved on to the Crown and Jewels, just off the High Street.

'No,' the woman said in response to the question as to whether she had a subscription or not. 'Subs would tie me down,' she said. 'I may look tied down, and in many ways the rest of my life is predictable, but not when it comes to choosing magazines. I came across Boulder Valley Business and Newts & Their Kind this week. Both very interesting reads.'

'But getting back to my original question,' the pub said.

'Oh dear, what was that? I think it was about why you

are not a great one for pubs. No, I tell a lie, that was not the question. You see I'm a bit doddery in the hearing and memory department,' the pub said. 'Too many years filled with crowds of men shouting, singing, competing with the tv. If there was a question I can't remember it. I am awash to the top of my spirits' optics with the echoes of past questions and responses, all mixed up and swirling around - turning into meaningless noise. But I have a question now. Did you ever work in a pub?'

'No,' the woman said. 'Never. What's it like?'

'You're asking the wrong entity, I have observed the impact it has on people, good and bad. What I have to endure is sticky carpets, ripped seats, blocked and vomit-stained toilets; otherwise I'm entirely passive. I just exist, I am, and will remain so long as there are enough drinkers to make it profitable for the brewery to keep me open, serving, alive. I'd hate to be knocked down, replaced by an apartment block. I don't want to be listed as special or historical or anything, just to be supported.'

'It's been lovely talking to you,' the woman said, 'but look at my fingers, they're twitching for a crochet project; a ball of wool and a needle — that's all I need, and I am happy. I have to get back to it; I might even try a Japanese doll, again. I wish you whatever you wish yourself, and I'm sure someone will come along to entertain you or whatever it is you want. And as I thought to say before, but didn't, I have a sense that talking pubs are either one of the world's best kept secrets or I am witnessing a first. But it's not making me comfortable.'

'Oh,' the pub said.

'I certainly don't want to be in next week's gazette with a double page spread of me talking to you, accompanied by a free CD featuring you answering me.'

'Maybe you have a prejudice towards engaging with community institutions.'

'Never, never, never – why, last week, I enjoyed what the fruit and veg shop had to say so much that I brought her home with me and we had fruit salad for days. She stayed for the weekend, and during that whole time I didn't once pick up a half-finished doily or as much as glance at my crochet needle and ball of wool. Not even once.'

An Unholy Night – K. L. Vincent

(Genre: Historical Fiction)

"Dead?"

The word trembled from Theodora's lips. She sat with her muslin handkerchief balled in her fist, her back stiff, trying not to touch the settee's cushioning.

"Pray, Mr. Rail. Did I hear you correctly?"

"Yes, I am afraid so." The Vicar's brow pulled tight, his manner in every way expressing sympathy. He had stumbled upon the man while returning from his evening sermon.

"Oh, not Papa! He left for his walk not yet an hour ago. How could this have happened?"

"We must wait for the Magistrate before leaping to any conclusions. I have already sent a missive." The Vicar clutched a proffered glass and sipped. "For now, we shall remain calm."

"The Magistrate?" George spun from the window. He had been watching the dark abyss of clouds that seemed to swallow the drawing room up, extinguishing the daylight. "Why do we need to involve the Magistrate?"

The Vicar took another sip. "It seems that Lord Ashworth—" His eyes skimmed to George. "The *late* Lord Ashworth…has been…" Another sip. "has been…"

"Out with it, Mr. Rail." George's fists clenched with impatience.

"He has been stabbed in the stomach."

Theodora gasped.

A snicker arose from the doorway. "The old fool deserved every wound inflicted upon him. I'm pleased he's dead."

"Julius! Why say such a thing? On the night of our father's death. It is a terrible thing to say, terrible. I feel I will faint from the shock of it. Hattie, Hattie!" Theodora flapped her handkerchief at a maid who had been silent until now.

"Miss?"

"Fetch my smelling salts."

"I have them here, Miss."

"You do? Of course you do. Bring them."

The slight maid, bending to Theodora's command, dashed over to administer the salts.

"Thank you, Hattie."

"Who could perform this act of brutality?" George settled on the armchair catty-corner of Theodora's settee.

Julius grinned. "I have no doubt one of us did the deed. To raise the knife and slash, a spill of crimson."

"Do not be vulgar, Brother, unless you would like to profess your own guilt."

"Me?" A laugh. "We all bear the marks of guilt. I have no motive for killing our old Rum Cull. And if it were I, I would not be so imprudent to admit it to you sorry lot."

Eyes flicked. Snivels and gulps from the rest punctured the stillness of Julius's accusation.

Hands wrung handkerchiefs. Was that a spot of blood on the cloth? Whose? From a bloody nose? Crying would do that.

Another on a lapel. The carelessness of carrying a wild pheasant rather than asking servants to do it.

Red nicks on a wrist? A nervous habit. The affliction of psoriasis commencing early in the season due to cold weather.

Outside, the storm manifested into a sudden and violent mass. The rain beat as the darkness advanced. Night transformed the room. Shadows gamboled, and corners grew ever more sinister. A scrape at the window.

Just a branch.

It brought attention to the display case of their father's hunting blades, the middle knife evidently missing.

How was this to be? Who from the Manor could possess the inclination and atrocity to murder Lord Ashworth?

They all glanced about, each civil, but realization dawned; one of them had. One had evolved into a devilish creature to commit this wicked act.

And what was to say it would not happen again?

To whom, then, did the guilt belong?

The room became taut with the scream of wind and flick of candle flame.

All eyes landed on one.

The missing knife grasped in their unholy hands.

Another Perfect Day, Dammit – Del Griffith

(Genre: Horror)

2075

Today is a great day for killing dead things. There are billions of them, and only a few of us.

Three figures close in on me, slow and clumsy. Original zombies, not like the later ones, who are fast, ruthless killing machines.

The heads come off quickly, bodies falling forward, spurts of black blood darkening the soil. I clean my machete, burn the bodies, smash the heads. Another productive day at the office.

ZETA, the Zombie Eradication and Training Academy, radios coordinates for a safe house. I make my way to Mater Divina Elementary School, climbing the stairs to the second floor and seeking a classroom that isn't overrun by rats.

Little chairs and low hooks adorn the classroom, now decades old. In the fading light, I circle the edges of the room, taking in the drawings still hanging on the walls. The kids who drew these are probably dead — or worse.

Bright reds, bold blues, and vibrant yellows, faded with time. Poorly-sketched families stand on rickety stick legs. Pets in abundance, with anything from two to seven legs. Abnormally large suns shining on abnormally small houses. A world only kids see.

A crackly, disembodied voice spills from my walkie. "Phoenix 131. Come in. We need a SITREP and a twenty."

"At the haven. Three down today. Over," I respond, my voice thick with fatigue.

"Be advised. Eaters in the area. Locals report five or six near the haven. Are you on the second floor?"

"Affirmative."

"Get some sleep and take them out tomorrow."

"Roger that. Out."

I unroll my sleeping bag and lay down, trying to clear my mind. I roll over and close my eyes, trying not to question why I have special blood, trying not to think about my wife, trying not to think about what tomorrow will bring. I swallow my sadness and anger, curl up into a ball, and concentrate on my breathing.

Eaters can't climb stairs, so I'm safe. I'm immune to their bites and scratches, thanks to the Phoenix antigen in my blood. But I'm not safe from the images flashing through my brain.

Sunday mornings, glowing like the walls of an Italian palazzo. Swirling mists over placid lakes. Vast sweeps of green in the countryside. My wife smiling at me, right before I cut her head off.

———

Sunlight streams in, through cracked blinds. I groan and sit up, drinking a half-liter of water and munching on blueberries. I finish my morning meal with smoked salmon. Killing Eaters requires a hearty breakfast.

Before the killing spree begins, I remove the drawings from the wall, carefully folding them and placing them in my bag, wedged between a whetstone and a bottle of antiseptic.

One Eater is at the foot of the stairs, its predatory gaze fixed on scurrying rats. It doesn't see me until I'm almost upon it, but by then it's too late. The head thuds on the floor.

Two more rush toward me. Fast ones. I back up, slashing at their heads, trying to avoid their powerful grips and slavering jaws. I push a chair in front of them and they stumble. I take off their heads with two clean slices before they can recover their balance. A near thing, and I'm shaken.

The last two lurch toward an exit, but their fate is sealed. Blood splatters the doors, a Jackson Pollock in organic material.

I drag the bodies outside and burn them under the jungle gym. I crush the heads and bury them in the sandbox.

2073

I get two days off per month, as long as I have double-digit kills. ZETA, if nothing else, knows how to motivate its soldiers.

I make my way home, relishing the thought of sleeping with Zoe, warm and safe in our bed, her murmurs of love thrilling me, taking me away from death and blood.

I walk in to a hug, and a kiss that says everything. My world, encapsulated by two arms and hungry lips.

Her arms, bruised and bleeding. Her lips, cracked, peeling, and dripping with spittle. A sigh, relegating the horror of our world to a place of permanent pain.

The signs are there, stark and unforgiving. She knows it

and I know it. We spend our final night together without saying much, but I can't stop touching her. In the morning, we go outside and kiss one last time. She doesn't taste like Zoe any longer.

She looks up at me from a kneeling position, smiling through tears, voice catching ever so slightly through slurred words.

"Aim true, sweetie."

I take off the head of the woman who is no longer my wife. That doesn't make it hurt any less.

***

2075

I head west from the school. When I hit the Pacific, I seal the drawings in bottles and let the immense blue waters determine their fate.

Four Eaters are wandering the beach. I dispatch them and sit on the sand, watching the sunset perform its magic.

It's another perfect day, dammit.

A small voice startles me. "Are you a Phoenix?"

The girl looks at me in awe, like I'm Santa Claus. I nod, too stunned to speak. I haven't seen a child in the open for years.

"Mom and dad are dead, those," she says, pointing at the four Eaters I have slain, "are the ones who killed them. I hid upstairs."

"I'm Sasha." The girl slips a small hand into mine.

She rummages around in a pocket with her other hand, pulling out half a green crayon, displaying it to me with pride. I sift through my bag and find the last letter my wife wrote to me. Three pages long, but a little space on the back page remains.

Sasha looks at the letter, frowning.

"What does it say?"

"It says" — I put an arm around her shoulder — "please draw me something in green."

Sasha proceeds to fill in the empty spaces of my life.

Another Reason I Can't Sleep at the Embassy – J.I. Mumford

(Genre: Sci-Fi)

To avoid incidents, the Diplomatic Corps uses local translators alongside our Terran team. We tediously describe a point in as many ways as practicable. When the exo-translators are certain they understand, they draft a document in their language. These are electronically translated back to Terran, compared with our originals, edited and annotated.

But last week, on a stack of newly printed technical manuals, I found a document printed in both Terran and Hoosh. Under our emblem, in the manner of all such small cheaply printed booklets produced by my department, was the title: NINE WAYS TO IDENTIFY YOUR SKIN.

Arthur – David McCahan

(Genre: Drama)

Arthur slipped into his grandmother's empty room, staring at the empty bed. He felt better being there. Sad, but better. Escaping the awkward family time at his grandmother's house, with the inevitable consolations, each sounding more contrived than the previous: "Now the healing begins"; "She's in a better place"; "She's at peace".

Arthur couldn't picture his grandmother being peaceful. Even at his young age, he'd recognized his grandmother as a nervous and sad person.

His last visit with her had been just three weeks earlier. She had been napping in her bedroom. Arthur's parents had taken the brief moment of peace to slip outside, leaving Arthur alone to watch his grandmother's chest rise and fall, her breath coming in long wheezing draws.

It startled him when she spoke.

"How long have you been there?" his grandmother asked.

Arthur didn't know. "A while," he said.

His grandmother began to cough, waving frantically for Arthur, who obligingly came to her bedside, his grandmother directing him to the nightstand and a glass of water that Arthur handed her. His grandmother, holding it with both hands, sipped with her eyes clenched shut.

A pause, a deep breath, relaxing as the cough subsided.

"Hand me my mirror," she instructed.

The small hand mirror lay on the stand next to the water,

a vase of gardenias, and a copy of the King James Bible.

Arthur watched his grandmother look into the mirror, her expression like she was staring at something far away, not just the reflection inches before her. She finally sighed and closed her eyes, pressing the mirror closer to her chest.

"Life goes so quickly." she said to no one in particular, and then to Arthur: "I was your age only yesterday."

Arthur didn't understand. He wasn't sure how old his grandmother was. He was told it was impolite to ask such things. But he was certain she'd been much older than seven yesterday.

"Look at yourself," his grandmother said, passing him her mirror. "Take a good look at yourself, Arthur."

Arthur again did as instructed. He saw his reflection, his blue eyes, dark hair, combed neatly, the small scratch on his left cheek he'd gotten from a tree branch the day before.

"Live in each moment, Arthur," his grandmother said. "It will all go by so fast."

He ran his hand over the mirror on the bed stand where he'd left it. Turning it over, he looked into it and remembered what his grandmother had said but didn't feel like this moment was one he particularly wanted to live in.

In his hand, his image in the mirror shimmered. He thought he'd imagined it. Then it happened again, and then it blurred, and the reflection was no longer of Arthur at age seven. It was Arthur, at least it resembled Arthur, but older now. In uniform. And looking confident.

Arthur shook his father's hand and kissed his mother's cheek. Swinging his bag over his shoulder, he headed to the car waiting to drive him to the train station and the train to San Francisco and the ship waiting there to take him overseas.

On the train, at night, the only one still awake, Arthur watched the dark shapes of the Nebraska fields whir by and wondered when and if he would ever get home. He wondered if he would ever see his parents again, his sister, his dog. Whether he would ever have a career or a family of his own, or if he would just join the constantly growing list of young men who would not.

Arthur dug around in his pack and found it. The mirror. He'd stolen it from his grandmother's bedside that morning of her funeral. He'd felt an attachment to it, to his grandmother through it. His talisman he never told anyone about.

He glanced at it, at his reflection in it. The train car provided just enough light to make out his features, but it was so dim that they appeared to alter with each jostle and bump of the tracks. His hair line began to recede, the corners of his eyes to crease, his forehead to wrinkle.

Arthur sat at his desk, a pile of overdue warehousing reports next to the formal portrait of his family. Arthur in his usual brown suit, his son in a similar version, mustard yellow shirts, matching orange and brown striped ties. His wife, bouffant hair freshly coiffed from the salon, his daughter in a handmade dress with zoo animals on it. Three of them smiled. Arthur just looked like he wanted the picture over with.

The phone rang. His wife needing him to stop at the market and pick up pork chops and a head of lettuce.

Arthur felt a grumble grow in him. He was exhausted. He just wanted to go home. How did this mundane errand fall upon him when he was out working fifty-hour weeks to provide that food for his family?

After dinner that night, when the house was asleep and Arthur was not, Arthur slipped from the bed and to the chest he kept in the basement. No one else had the key but him. It contained the remnants of the life before now. Jar of marbles, Boy Scout sash, Navy uniform, and his grandmother's mirror.

In the dust of the basement illuminated by the bare bulb in the fixture overhead, Arthur looked again into the mirror, hoping for something better. Whether that better existed in his future or was left in his past, he wasn't certain. He just hoped.

And the reflection that remained was that of an old man, blue blazer, striped tie, bifocals, his head almost completely bald save a thin gray rim around the edge. He looked like he was smiling, for Arthur. For many people it would have appeared he was only trying to not not smile.

In his small apartment in the retirement home, Arthur looked at the wall of pictures over his breakfast table. Faded black-and-whites of his parents, his childhood, his time in the service.

Once bright Kodachromes of his wedding, his early years with his wife, his early years with his children, the color bleaching out over years along with Arthur's expression. Then only pictures of him with his wife and daughter. And then only with his daughter.

Arthur looked at his grandmother's mirror in his hand

and wondered where the time had gone.

His daughter caught her father's arm and mirror before either crashed onto the bedstand. She lay the mirror safely to the side and Arthur's arm comfortably back across his chest.

Arthur's breath came in deeper gasps, longer gaps between them. And then it stopped.

"Dad?" his daughter asked.

Seven-year-old Arthur stood behind his daughter, watching her cry on the old man in the bed.

He turned back to look over his shoulder as a gentle hand rested upon it.

His grandmother, younger than he remembered her ever being, looked down on him and smiled.

"I told you," she said. "It all goes so quickly."

At the Top of the World – Robert Burns

(Genre: Drama)

Where the top of the world meets the sky, snowy crystalline mist takes wing, reflecting rainbow prisms of color into the clearest cobalt blue ever seen. This is where God speaks to climbers for the first—sometimes last—time.

Aaron lay in fetal position, watching the sun set through horizontal eyes, as celestial streets of fire reflected off distant slopes. He didn't hurt anymore.

It was Emily's voice—not God's—that beckoned him home, though. They stood in warm golden sand, gentle sea breeze caressing their faces. She tossed Aaron the beach ball, spinning red and yellow and cobalt blue.

Away the Governor – J.I. Mumford

(Genre: Fairytale)

The Governor grew weary from many faithful years of spinning over his metal city.

The engineers pulled the bronze disks from his neck and laid him bare, arms akimbo. Sick and cold, in half dream, sticky from old oil.

The eccentric rods, pleased with their reprieve, said, "You pushed us too hard, and to your own ruin!"

The cross head, who was rarely cross, stared at its slippers.

The pistons—usually chatty and kind, said, "Swinging your balls in the air all day isn't terribly becoming of...well, it's just not done."

At this, the Governor said, "Only cowards insult dying majesty."

Basic Make-Up Steps – Alexis Araneta

(Genre: Romance)

1. Prime her alabaster skin so that the oils do not show once she's out and her girlfriends see her.

2. Apply foundation to cover up the freckles she had always despised but that you could never resist leaving little pecks on.

3. Highlight and contour her fox-like face to make the cheeks you had kissed a thousand times — in bed, in the shower, in your favourite restaurant — pop.

4. Paint her lids the vibrant blues and greens of your wedding motif, the same one she gleefully chose when you put a diamond on her finger.

5. Buff her cheeks with the rose flush of your undulating bodies intertwining passionately every night for the past seven years.

6. Swipe her luscious lips with the bright berry lipstick she always left on your pristine white shirts after every date night ended with you two cuddling on the couch.

7. Once you're done with prepping her, try not to let the guilt crash over you like a tidal wave as you remember having been on the other side of town for work when she drowned.

Better Living Through Chemicals – Deidra Whitt Lovegren

(Genre: Drama)

"If you're going to hold a knife to my throat, then use it," the old woman mutters, as the young man clutches her head in the crook of his arm. "But before you hurt me, would you like some coffee?"

He nods, releasing her. She hands him a steaming ceramic mug.

As he sips, she notices his breathing slows. Antipsychotic medications tended to work quickly.

"Mom—" he sobs. "I promise! I took my meds…"

"I know you tried to, son. Let's see how this one works." She puts her worn hands on his shoulders, her worn heart in her throat.

Between the Black and White – Kay Northbridge

(Genre: Drama)

Water gushes over the windscreen in waves as unrelenting as my grief. The streetlights are blurry starbursts in my struggling vision.

Black clouds hang with menaces above, banishing celestial light from view. The bottle bangs my teeth, even at this low speed. But the bourbon tastes like freedom spilling over my tongue.

'It's like dancing at the end of the rain,' she'd say. But only when she was sky-high happy. I never danced with her. The rigidity of my nerves and the well-structured failure of my confidence built a prison around me. I never even tried to escape.

I promised, in her final days, as time and options drained away, that we would dance. She smiled, touched my cheek and said, 'I never needed you to be anyone else.'

Since the day I placed a rose on her coffin, I have puked self-loathing every morning. Wracked with regret and apologies she will never hear.

I've never seen the end of the rain. Only an occasional merging of droplets and air that wet my face and left me damp, disappointed.

She often told a story of how she saw it once, as a kid, in a windless field. How the drops fell like a curtain on the corn. How she stepped forward, out of the cloud cover, and was no longer getting wet. The edge of the rain still visible, a shining wall of tiny prisms in the morning sun.

She held out a hand and touched the tears of heaven. She was no longer standing in it. She was no longer standing at all. Spinning and stretching, turning and twirling, bowing and bending. Dancing at the end of the rain.

Her lithe steps took her between worlds: one wet, one dry, one black, one white. But I knew she lived for the grey, the beautiful greys of life.

Just once in her time had she seen this marvel. But it stayed with her, like a loyal dog. The memory bounded after her through the towering high rises of her childhood, along the busy streets to school. It accompanied her around the green university campus and down the dull corridors of her office block. It followed her to our wedding and watched while she danced with her father instead of her groom.

I never understood why she loved me, and I was too scared to ask. Maybe testing her would break us. But those words flowed from her mouth with the ease of a swallow in flight. She told me often as she looked deep into my dark brown eyes, her blue-grey irises like a storm, glinting with mischief. Sometimes she'd toy with her flaxen hair, knowing it would stir me, and we wouldn't emerge from our blissful coupling for an hour or so.

Another car sounds its piercing horn. I'm over the line. I clumsily emerge from my daydream and a moment of cold runs through me. But memories are all I have. Memories and a gold band on my finger. And a promise.

I take another swig from my bottle of freedom and it warms me through. It tastes like our first date at the steakhouse.

A lightning flash illuminates the road. Skeletal trees

come into sharp relief and sear into my vision when I blink. Like a burned-on memory. Memories and promises are all I have.

The storm is huge and unmoving. It's not often they come with such little wind, to hang around like an uninvited guest. But this one is here to stay, for a little while.

A few minutes more and there it is. In the clear sky ahead, stars are revealed like flecks of glitter on a sugar-paper ceiling. My moment is coming. Her moment. Our moment.

The rain hasn't stopped, I've just reached the end of it, driven through the magical gateway. I pull over onto the verge and grab the silver urn from the passenger side, holding it firmly to my chest. 'Why such a sorrowful shape?' her mother had asked. But we knew, didn't we? We knew it wasn't a tear, it was a raindrop. A beautiful symbol of your happiest time.

I get out of the car and shut the door. There's a five-bar gate separating me from the field. It's not raining on my bit of verge, but it is raining behind the car. I'm finally here.

Droplets from the gate soak through my jeans, cold accusations against my thighs as I trespass onto the farmland.

She was right. Even in the dark, this is an extraordinary sight. The edge of the rain, the fringe of the storm, the place with no grey area. You're in or you're out. Unless you dance.

My torchlight reflects off the downpour, showing me the border. Showing me the dancefloor. I twirl. A smile spreads across my eyes before my lips catch up. I brush a tear from my cheek, or was it a raindrop? My feet are finding their rhythm, finding their timing, finding their beat. My shirt sleeves stick to my arms, water trails down my neck.

I open the lacquered urn and shake it away from me. She begins to leave her aluminium jail as I begin to leave the confines of my insecurities.

Only she can see me in the dark. I move between the wet and dry, the black and white.

I spin and stretch, turn and twirl, bow and bend. I don't need music; she's singing to me. Her dull ashes spill into the rain, onto the field. She is the beautiful grey between the black and white.

I keep my promise and we dance together for the very first time.

Between Stars and Silence – Míriam Toyama

(Genre: Sci-Fi)

He feels like he is floating. He feels something after a very long time, it seems. He opens his eyes and doesn't believe what he sees. Stars are exploding, worlds are dying, and the sky is beautiful and lit with so many exploding suns. 'Is it really a sky if you are standing in the middle of it?' he thinks.

"Where are we? Who are you?" He can see a tall man, with empty black eyes and a disinterested face.

"The edge of everything; life is about to become impossible. And from here on it's going to be quieter till it starts all over again," says the man, who seems to be floating, just like him.

"I don't understand…"

"No, I suppose you don't. Your ship thing, it broke, but it kept you. You were frozen in time, drifting in space."

"Am I dead?" Exasperation starts showing in his voice.

"No. The ship thing. It kept you alive," the man says, punctuating every word.

"Oh, and who are you?"

"Nobody."

"No, I mean what's your name? Where did you come from?"

"You can choose a name."

"That's not how it works. Where is everybody else?"

"They are dead; you're the last one. Are you paying attention?" He seems genuinely concerned.

"What? Everybody?" The man is despairing.

"Like I said before, you are the last one."

"What do you mean? You said life…" Confusion infuses his voice.

"Life as you know is ending. The Universe will follow its cycle; it will eventually be reborn into something shiny and new. Now the last trees are withering down, suns are exploding, and so on. You, the last living human, will die soon. Your ship thing is about to break."

"I'm on the ship?"

"You're having a hard time following this, aren't you? Yes, your body is; your consciousness is here with me. I thought you would like to see it. I thought someone should see it."

"But I don't want to die!" His voice rises a little.

"I know. Humans never want to die. Why is that? Can you tell me? You know, everything dies, it's inevitable. It's the way things are."

"But I had a whole life in front of me! The ship! The ship is full… so many people. My wife, my wife is on the ship! Is she…?"

"You are the last one."

"We were moving, seeking a better life. She wanted to have kids. She wanted them and I said… I said we should wait until we settle, have more money, more space. We should wait till we arrived in the new place," he says, fidgeting with his hands.

"Mm... Living seems complicated when you're the one living; from afar it just seems like everything would resolve quicker if you all communicated better, even when you don't know all the variables in a situation."

"Now we'll never have kids!"

"If it's any consolation, no one will have kids. There will be no kids for a while. Maybe next time life will find another way to evolve, to organize itself."

"What? No kids? That would be a shame…"

"Mm, I suppose. They are adorable," he says with a light smile.

"So I'll die?"

"Yes."

"And you?"

"I'm not technically alive."

"No? What are you then?"

"Just an observer."

"An observer? And you brought me here, to observe the end with you? Will you end too?"

"No. I continue to observe. I will wait. And life will reappear, will rearrange itself. And I will be here to see. As this cycle ends, I thought a human should be present. You are the last one. I thought you should see it. I thought you would want to see it. This time you all expanded so much, you created so many beautiful things and so many terrible ones. You blessed each other with grace and love. And you cursed each other with hate and power. You lived, and you created; you all did so much, and now it all reaches an end. I thought at least one of you should see it.”

“It is kind of beautiful in a bittersweet way, you know. I had a life, a good one I think; I loved and was loved. But what now? What happens to me?”

“To be honest, I don’t know where you go now. I’ve seen it happen before. I can tell you what I’ve observed throughout the time. It’s usually peaceful if you don’t try to control it. Some even smile in the end. Those who follow the flow of things, well, those seem to be happier. I wouldn’t recommend trying to stick around. It would be lonely. Especially lonely for you.”

“Do I get to see my wife again?”

“I hope you can. I hope you get the chance to see all your loved ones. Just like some of you used to believe.”

“And you? You stay here? Alone?”

“I’m just an observer. I register all that happens. That is my purpose, just like yours is to live. It will be quiet for a while, still beautiful, but quiet. Then the next thing will come and I will be here, watching, registering, and caring.”

“But why?”

“Someone should care when things die, when civilizations collapse and rise again. Someone should care when good living beings cease to exist. And just as well, someone should be there for the shiniest sunrise and witness when love comes to be. That’s what I do. It all should leave a mark. More than that, I want to be here and witness it all. I’m grateful that I can.”

“That’s good, I think. You are right, of course. Someone should care, I think. About life and beauty, and all of those things… I'm not sure what's happening; I'm getting sleepy."

"Your body is calling you back. Don't worry. I'll go with you. I will watch over you. It will be okay," is the last thing said in a while as everything quiets down.

Biography of a Tree – Hannah P. Simmons

(Genre: Sci-Fi)

I better start with the tree. Nothing makes sense if you don't know about the little tree.

Things don't live for very long here. Or, they don't *grow* for very long. It's not that they stop growing, we just don't give them *time*. Especially trees. We have lots of them, but they aren't very tall. Well, alright, they are *tall* as far as trees go, I guess. But they are only allowed to grow SO tall before they are harvested and new ones are planted.

There's a story that, at one time, trees just grew. No one was watching for them, waiting for them. They just grew. They kept growing and growing for as long as they wanted. They kept reaching, higher and higher. They weren't afraid, because no one was watching for them, waiting for them.

Sometimes, it's very hard for me to believe that story. But I want to believe it. Who wouldn't want to believe in a world where trees can just be there *because*? But when every business has a crew of harvesters, it's hard to conceive. Everything must be harvested.

Vegetable. Animal. Mineral. That's how we have continued to survive. Each piece of earth must be functional.

So we harvest the trees.

One year, the harvesters missed a tree. It was hidden.

No, it was *hiding*.

It made itself as small as possible, behind some rocks. When the harvesters came, the little tree held its breath. It listened while all the others were taken. It was very hard to listen. It was very painful. But the little tree kept quiet and hidden 'til it was all over. And so, it was left behind.

When the harvesters were gone, the tree could breathe again. It took deep breaths, it GULPED the air! And it grew. It kept growing and growing. Reaching higher and higher, because it wasn't afraid anymore. Because by the time the harvesters would return, it wouldn't matter. Once you have your moment touching the sky, they can't take that away.

When I found the tree, it had already had its moment in the sky. It made me wonder what it's like. To reach higher than they said you could.

Breakfast With Alice – Robert Burns

(Genre: Drama)

The edges of the egg turn milky, opaque. Curling in the pan, they sizzle, pop in the grease.

Alvie studies the sunny yolk.

Alice usually cooks.

He pokes at it with the spatula. Sunshine bleeds into clouds.

Through the window, the forest behind the house beckons. He stares into the dark, crooked pines. Numb.

The last time I saw her, we ran hand in hand through the woods to the little crystal stream. We made love.

The shrieking smoke detector pulls Alvie back. Snatching the pan, he dumps burnt egg into the trash.

He sighs, reaches for the carton.

Empty.

Bumbling Through the Bzzt Bop – April Pereira

(Genre: Comedy)

Noah's grip crushed the alien dictionary, its indecipherable glyphs blurring before his eyes. The Bzzt's iridescent wings fluttered as he finished his final, fluid twirl.

Noah's stomach lurched — his turn. "Easy," he'd assured the interviewers, brimming with misplaced confidence about his fluency in extraterrestrial languages.

Why didn't anyone mention the Bzzt communicated through dance?

Hesitant, Noah lunged, performing a clumsy imitation of the spin. The Bzzt tilted his head, antennae twitching, before erupting into a series of high-pitched chirps resembling laughter. Then, he launched into another pirouette, beckoning Noah to join. Noah gulped. Maybe 'easy' was a relative term.

Charms and Arabesque – April Pereira

(Genre: Fantasy)

Flour dusted Lúcia's cheeks like fairy kisses as she simmered the infusion. Her kitchen was an alchemist's lab of bubbling concoctions and precise measurements. *Lavender for confidence. Passionflower and jasmine to enhance attraction.*

With effortless pirouettes and a quicksilver smile, Alis belonged to another world – one of silk leotards and glistening barre workouts. They were as different as a witch's cauldron from fine china. Yet, warmth bloomed in Lúcia's chest, spreading like the scent of simmering herbs, as she recalled the music of Alis's voice discussing arcane symbolism after class.

Tonight, during the studio's annual showcase, she would weave magic into her steps. Lúcia secured a rosemary charm onto her costume, a symbol of passion according to the ancient grimoires. A mischievous glint entered her eyes as she sipped the potion and imagined Alis catching the subtle message.

***

A vision of grace in turquoise, Seraphina, Alis's partner, executed every leap and plié with effortless elegance. Lúcia's breath hitched as Seraphina glided across the floor and into Alis's arms for a lift. A pang of envy, sharp and unwelcome, twisted in her gut.

When Lúcia's turn came, she took a deep breath and stepped forward. There was a murmur in the audience. Her costume — a patchwork of swirling skirts hand-stitched with charms — was in blatant defiance of the ballet theme.

The music pulsed, a primal rhythm mirroring her pounding heart. With each twirl, Lúcia felt the magic bloom. This was hers — raw, powerful, a primal echo in her very bones. A flicker of movement in the corner of her eye caught her attention. Seraphina, captivated, swayed to the rhythm, her eyes fixed on Lúcia. A surge of exhilaration washed over her, chasing away the last vestiges of doubt. This was her dance, a wild symphony claiming the stage. She wouldn't be invisible any longer.

Lúcia twirled faster, her movements echoing the stirring pot in her kitchen. This wasn't just dance, but a potent mix of raw energy and kitchen magic. As she reached the climax, she threw her head back and sang, the words barely audible but infused with power.

Alis began to move in sync with Lúcia, a liquid counterpoint to her wildness. Drawn in, Seraphina's ballet slippers whispered on the wooden floor as she joined the dance. Together, they were a captivating whirlwind — Lúcia's earthy energy blending with Seraphina's ethereal grace and Alis's rippling movements. When the music ended, the applause was thunderous.

***

Alis's eyes met hers, wonderment glowing in their depths. "That was amazing."

Seraphina added, "It was like you bottled the magic of dance itself."

Lúcia felt a kaleidoscope of emotions bloom in her chest. Their dance, fueled by her magic and raw emotion, had unveiled a truth — she wasn't invisible. She was powerful, captivating, and worthy of connection. A slow smile spread across Lúcia's face as she met Alis's gaze, then flicked to Seraphina, whose playful nudge and impish smile spoke volumes.

"Pizza?" Lúcia suggested with an uplifted brow, her voice brimming with newfound confidence.

Cheap Labor – J.I. Mumford

(Genre: Fantasy)

Hunched on a dusty bench, the old man scratches at a weeping sore on his leg, his gaze lost in the distant blur of traffic. Flies dance, ruffle and spread with the gusts of wind, only to settle once more to sample a stain on his threadbare shirt, salt on his cheek, muck on his shoes.

The man's hands are gnarled and cracked, as if roots pulled from solid earth. His eyes, twin wells of amber, hold the sediment of countless dawns. His face, a map of countless dusks, the creases carving deeper with each passing year. If one looked closely, they might read the dirt-caked chapters of his story etched into his leathered skin. Laugh lines are missing from the crags over his cheeks, the skin merely wrinkled at the corners of his eyes. There, you will only find the sadness of being alone in the world; for he is old—old enough to have chained Death to avoid his own demise.

To the hurried pedestrians, cocooned in their technology, he is but a smudge on the city's polished facade—a ghost of a man, easily dismissed and forgotten. Though their shoes are dulled with the same grey powder.

Approach—he is harmless.

There is a muted vulnerability about him, that of obsolescent antiquity, as that of a discarded tin cup or broken pipe found on the banks of a river. He carries no malice, only his story, and he freely gifts it to any with patience.

One will hear the mud on his face crack as he recounts his adventures: "Often the hero's stories end at the conclusion of the epic, not of the hero." Here he raises himself up. "Your heroes, if they survived their journey, drift into mediocrity." He waves his fingers in a manner that only happens once in his retelling. Fine powder falls from where his knuckles brush. "You may have heard of such a hero. This hero was a clever and mighty king. He had near boundless wealth and lived in comfort as reward for his heroic deeds."

Here he shrinks. His back returns to the curve of an ancient. "However, this king, though a righteous act—" he taps his knot-wood cane for each word "—killed a visitor to his city." His cane stills, only to be tapped again if he sees one's attention wander. "The old gods, being without reason or pity, sent the king away to a mountain."

Dust will fall from his threadbare shirt. Dried mud will flake from his rheumatic hands. Throughout his story, detritus floats or falls. Large clumps fall as to their size as he gesticulates at the peaks. He continues, "Those old gods are all gone, and their towers dust. Time moves on and friction takes its toll. Granite wears, and the heart of the mountain is long since powdered."

Stand firm.

Others will rush by, to avoid the acrid filth of his tattered clothing. They suspect his story is as old as the village… and quietly joke that the man is as old as the valley where he now spreads dust at your feet. Ignore them; listen to the old man.

Never mind how his spittle congeals with dust under his lip or drips into his patchy beard. His recounting of eternity is not much to tell. From his heyday to the present, much is toil left unrepeated. He has done nothing ignoble since his last sin. His memories are mostly the sadness of living in mediocrity.

Stay mute.

Raising a hand to him, or begging his pardon, will add the novelty of your name to his story; he has a long memory. Worse, if he loses his place, he will start his story again. Restarting his task has never been too much of a climb. It is, as Hades would appreciate, a task in spirit if not action.

When his monologue rolls to a rest, with his gravel and syrup voice, the loquacious old fart will quote Camus:

"A face that toils so close to stones is already stone itself."

From then on, he will be of use.

He is a fair labourer, most at peace when working on mindless tasks with a heavy burden. His sagging skin covers metal-tight muscle; to touch his arm would be to feel a cable-stayed bridge wrapped in a sheet of cotton. This man is a completionist, and will climb any mound, with any weight, for as long as the task requires. He is also cheap labour, on account of him being so ancient. He will work for shoes—and a flat place to rest his boulder.

In a valley of those obsessed with the promise of immortality, his is the solitary, ancient, heartbeat. Gazing out at a world that has long since forgotten him as a hero, he waits to tell you his story. His mountain ground to dust, Sisyphus sits in the valley, scratching at his sore.

Chemistry Experiment – Cristina Rose Strube

(Genre: Romantic Comedy)

Roughly half an hour was left of class, and Professor Nguyen was just about through grading all of the midterm exams from a week ago. He took a last glance over Max's paper, filled out in the young man's typical succinct manner - Max hated using more words than he deemed necessary, which was usually fewer than his professors required of him. '94% Good work, thesis needs elaboration.' Professor Nguyen wrote across the top of the paper.

Adjusting his bifocals, Professor Nguyen glanced up at his class, most of whom were wrapping up the assigned chemistry experiment. The last three individuals were Erica - staring in horror at her blank worksheet - and the team of Justin and Heidi, who seemed to be engrossed in something he hadn't assigned.

"Justin and Heidi seem to be performing a little experiment of their own," the professor announced loudly; the students in question quickly jumped away from each other and their previous activity.

"Sorry, sir," Justin apologized awkwardly, pulling at a t-shirt that didn't need straightening in a desperate attempt to draw attention to anywhere other than where it was at the moment.

"That's quite all right." Professor Nguyen grinned mischievously. "After all, you two do have chemistry together, and what you were doing was a sort of experiment. I'd like you to demonstrate it in front of the class."

"No thank you, Professor Nguyen." Heidi smiled disarmingly, as if trying to wriggle her way out of the impending humiliation.

"Yes, right now." Professor Nguyen responded in a calm, assertive voice. "And don't stop until I tell you. I'd like to take the opportunity to give your peers a lecture on the very topic."

Not making any further attempt to persuade their professor otherwise, Justin and Heidi reluctantly leaned into a kiss, seeming to enjoy this one much less than the one they'd thought they'd shared sneakily mere minutes before.

"You might be wondering why I'm taking time out of your lessons to have you watch your classmates kiss." Professor Nguyen deliberately spoke slowly - wishing to drag out his students' psychological torture. This was his way of making sure they would take care not to be off task in his class ever again.

"But kissing is truly, at its heart, science - where chemistry and biology intersect. You see... while these matters are hardly ever what is going through your conscious mind the first time you kiss someone new, what your instincts are really doing is testing to see if that person would be suitable to be the other parent to your future children. At this point, small receptors in Justin's and Heidi's lips are passing hormones back and forth as a way of communicating on a subconscious level. These hormones - a type of natural chemical, mind you - then travel up to their brains, where they will be interpreted in one of a few ways.

"If Justin and Heidi are currently registering disgust, and they can't wait for me to tell them they can part -

not because they're embarrassed but because they have a horrible taste in their mouths - that means they are not genetically compatible whatsoever. If they had a kid together, there is a good chance that child would be inflicted with some sort of recessive genetic disease. Their bodies are practically screaming at them, 'Get away from this creature immediately, and don't you dare even think of letting it mate with you! Future generations will be doomed if you do!'

"If Justin and Heidi are experiencing a mildly pleasant sensation from the kiss, it means an offspring of theirs wouldn't have any particularly spectacular attributes. Their bodies are saying, 'Eh, you could use this one for passing on your DNA if there isn't anything better. Keep looking, though; you'll never have kids that are ahead of the game if you stay here.'

"Then there is the possibility that fireworks are going off in their brains right now, declaring that this is the most marvelous thing their lips have ever touched. If that is the case, their DNA is just about a perfect match for each other. Justin's strongest traits meld exactly to the places where Heidi's are lacking, and vice versa. Their child would likely be either a genius or a star athlete, something that would give it an advantage in surviving to adulthood and passing on its own genetics. That doesn't assure that they would be happy in a relationship together, mind you; talking determines that far better than kisses, but if you ever want to know if you could have beautiful children with someone - kiss them! Thank you, you two, you may end your demonstration."

Justin and Heidi gasped for air, presumably relieved to have their mouths reassigned to that task after what must have seemed like an eternity of being allowed to breathe only through their noses. Both blushed furiously as if unable to rid their imaginations of their hypothetical baby that Professor Nguyen had brought into being.

"So what's the verdict?" a classmate called out.

"Decline to state," Justin coughed.

Come Away – Beth Connor

(Genre: Fantasy)

Under an ashen sky, mourners gathered around a tiny grave, the scent of wet earth mingling with the whispers of a life cut short. Finn stood apart, his small hands clenched, staring at the soil that covered his sister, Aisling. His parents clung to each other, faces pale with grief. Gran, eyes fixed downward, drew her shawl tight against the chill.

The priest's voice droned, offering prayers of peace. Finn brushed the cold, damp headstone with his fingers, Aisling's name etched deep into his heart. As the service ended, the congregation dispersed, each lost in their reflections on life's unfairness.

Finn tugged at his mother's sleeve. "I'm hungry. Can we have lunch?"

She stared blankly. His da shook her gently. "The others will gather at the house, dear," he said, voice trembling.

"I can't," she murmured, fighting tears. "I won't leave her alone."

The ride home was silent. Finn wished Aisling were there to make him laugh. At home, a sea of black-clad relatives filled the house, too lost in their grief to notice Finn weaving between them.

Outside, the sun emerged, burning away the morning's darkness. Finn slipped out to the old swing hanging from the ancient oak. As he swung, he recalled the laughter he and Aisling had shared.

A glimmer among the flowers caught his eye—a fleeting

light in the cowslips. Gran noticed and called out, "Come along, A leanbh, it is not a time to be alone."

Reluctantly, Finn followed. Inside, his mother seemed somewhat revived, busying herself with the guests. Finn approached her, trying to be polite. "Can we play, Mum?"

Her face shadowed with sorrow. "Not today, my sweet child," she managed.

That night, Finn gazed at the empty bed where Aisling had slept, the rocking chair between them now silent. The moon cast a glow through his window as he wished to feel happy again. He could almost hear his sister's voice calling, "Come away... Come away and play."

The next morning was much the same. Finn asked his da to build a fort, but his da looked through him, seeing something else. "Perhaps another time."

A flicker of movement caught Finn's eye—a tiny creature with a red hat darted across the room, almost person-like. But it vanished before he could investigate.

That night, Finn asked Gran for a story. "No stories tonight, my dear. These bones are old and tired," she replied. Finn slid into Aisling's bed, squeezing his eyes shut and wishing for happiness.

This time, the voice was unmistakable. "Come away... Come away and play with us." Finn crept to the window. In the moonlight stood a diminutive figure with a face like a hedgehog's, wearing a coat and tiny boots. Finn stifled a squeal of delight and tiptoed outside.

Cool grass brushed his bare feet. The night air, alive with laughter, enveloped him. He encountered a circle of small ones, their eyes twinkling like stars. Together, they played under the moon's silver glow, darting through fields.

The small ones gathered around Finn, their faces alight. They reached out delicate hands, beckoning him to join them in a land untouched by sorrow. Finn looked back at his house, now more a shell than a home, where grief darkened the windows.

"Come away, O human child," they whispered. "To the waters and the wild."

Finn saw his family wrapped in their cloaks of sadness. They did not need him to share their mourning. "The world's more full of weeping than you can understand," the faeries sang.

Finn felt a deep calm. With these friends, he could be happy and play forever. "Away with us, he's going," the wind whispered through the trees.

Under the moon's silver glow, Finn danced and played, feeling neither sadness nor loneliness. Without looking back, he skipped hand in hand with the little hedgehog man.

"Away with us he's going," his new friends sang as they waded through pools, pushing the rushes aside. "For the world is more full of weeping than he can understand."

Cottonmouth Stew – Deidra Whitt Lovegren

(Genre: Drama)

A Cajun girl will only take a beating for so long.

I tell Lucien as much before he orders Delphine to fill our bellies, slapping her when she says there ain't nothing to eat.

"Plenty of vittles in the swamp!"

While she's out scavenging, we get drunk on the filthy couch.

She returns with a tubful of snakes. Soon, our stomachs growl at the melding of onion, garlic, and paprika. We eat in the kitchen while she picks up our beer cans and fluffs the couch's pillows.

Soon, we learn two truths: angry women and hidden snakeheads are both deadly.

Daemonicus Anonymous – J.I. Mumford

(Genre: Comedy)

"Welcome. I'm the group leader, Paul. Angie, since you're new, why don't you start this meeting of Demonicus Anonymous by telling us about your manifestation?"

"Okies! Hi, I'm Angie and this is Yog-So-Soft."

"Hi Angie!"

"He's so pink and fluffy and I love him soooo much! I hug him, and squeeze his cute little cheeks, and we have tea parties every day!"

"Thank you for sharing. Remember, we're here to help."

"Also, my mom said cookies aren't good for mister Softy's bott bott, and Mummie won't let me feed him any more neighbours. So now I'm here…he's very hungry."

Darkness – Daniel R. Hayes

(Genre: Drama)

"In the curvature of its depths, so warm, so gentle. The colors are bright and beautiful, but the winds of life are strong and powerful. I can't make sense of things. Keeping hope for the sake of hope. Holding onto faith because that's what you're supposed to do. Watching angels cry, powerless to intervene. Can anyone hear me? So, it's down to this. After a long, hard fall. The sun's rays no longer tickle my flesh, and winter's kiss steals my soul. Darkness is all I can see, and darkness I shall come to love."

Dendroid – K. L. Vincent

(Genre: Sci-Fi)

"By 'life,' we mean a thing that can nourish itself and grow and decay." – Aristotle

The trees call. Are they tracking me like the others?

Yellow mist stretches, encasing branches and saturating leaves. Its steady drip drowns the sharp yips and whistles beyond the forest's edge. I must keep moving. Perhaps the jungle and its tangle will devour my body, eating me whole before the others find me.

Let it. I'd rather be eaten than spend a life in the laboratory.

A wound gnaws at my side like a dog's teeth on bone. I ignore it. If I dwell on the pain, I won't move. And I have to move. The wound oozes red liquid. It seeps through cloth, leaving a trail for those howling to find.

It is blood, but it is not mine—not really. Blood is just a part of this shell I inhabit. It sustains my body, but it is not *me*.

Streaks of it stain the endless shades of green.

Nothing in the laboratory possessed a color so alive. There, only steel, glass, and shine exist. This green smells of water from their faucets, but without the metallic bite. It is wild, a wild so unfamiliar I want to combust.

My feet ache. I pause for breath. Those who chase me have paused, too. It is quiet. No, not quiet: unknown. My ears register new sounds. Birds?

Soft earth cushions my soles.

They once brought a green thing into the laboratory: a thin stem shot from a rich, dark earth, the same that covers my feet. It looked like a straw in a cup. I burrow my toes into the ground. I am that tiny plant trying to survive the unknown.

Have I adapted? Or do I stand out like the artificial being I am?

I am incompatible.

I have no history like this forest. The roots around me sink deep. Their age surpasses my own. A machine has no roots, no ground to hold into.

An image of the plant flashes before me, snapped in half and dead, its earth arid and crumbled on the polished floor. My feet move again. I am not changing. I will be no more than that plant in the laboratory, broken and dead.

I don't belong. An experiment doesn't belong in a forest.

My breath hitches, and the mist seeps into my lungs. I drink it in, moisture soaking the air sacs like leaves.

Is it not all an experiment? This forest took longer to grow, but do I not live and breathe, like this wild place?

Thorns prick my reflective skin. I want to be real. It's why I ran.

I stop and listen. The whistles no longer whine. A response blooms inside, swelling like ink in water. It bursts from the hole at my side. Something coils across my foot—a root. I am found.

Deity – Suma Jayachandar

(Genre: Romance)

You say

I reside

Deep in the sanctum

Of your heart

Like a reigning deity

The object of your utter devotion

I say

Please let me out

Of those confines

And show me

How you care

For I'm not made of stone or silver

I'm just a human, like you

*Drama at the Country Women's Association –
Michelle Oliver*

(Genre: Drama)

Miss Eileen Watterson smoothed her pretty pink gloves over gnarled fingers and adjusted the narrow brim of her cloche hat. For fifty-two years, she'd taken the trophy at the CWA Best in Bloom Competition. Fifty-two blue ribbons upon her mantle, and she was poised to collect number fifty-three. She cast a critical eye over her entry. The marigolds bloomed in a symmetrical fashion, just as they had every year. She was proud of their vivid colours. The trophy was all but hers.

Next to her, Betty Jameson placed a potted gardenia. The waxy leaves on the evergreen shrub glistened. Betty brought the same bush year after year, and although the flower was sweet, it inevitably had a brown spot or two. Poor Betty didn't understand the commitment required to curate the perfect bloom. It was why no trophy adorned Mrs Jameson's mantle. However, year after year she brought the sorry plant to the show.

"Ladies and gentlemen, it's time to announce the winner of this year's Best in Bloom competition," Ray Reynolds declared. Until last year, Ray's father had presided over the judging, but Patrick Reynolds had passed away. Heart attack. So sad; he'd only been seventy-three.

Young Ray approached the tables, where an abundance of blooms filled the air with an assortment of scents. He wandered past Anne Lasonby's petunias, past Gillian Eggelton's roses, past Sylvia Trivic's unusual offering this

113

year, *Trollius europaeus*, commonly known as 'globe flower'. But every entry paled when compared with Eileen's marigold. She waited, the perfect smile upon her lips. Waited for the ribbon to land upon her pot.

The crowd gasped as Ray stepped past her potted plant. He didn't even pause. Eileen's left eyelid fluttered, and she pressed her lips together, squeezing her hands to prevent them from trembling. Ray was a showman, unlike his no-nonsense father. He was playing to the audience, building suspense, adding a bit of 'Reality TV' drama. Young people these days liked the anticipation, the buildup, the tension. He would spin this moment out, he would…

… place the ribbon on Betty Jameson's gardenia!

Eileen's mouth dropped open.

"I beg your pardon, young Ray. You've placed the ribbon incorrectly."

"There's no mistake, Miss Watterson. The judge's decision is final."

"But… my marigold… it's a far superior bloom."

"Miss Watterson, your marigold is quite fine… for a marigold. But have you smelled this gardenia?" He turned his nose to one imperfect bloom and inhaled. "Heavenly."

Miss Eileen Watterson grasped her precious pot and clutched the perfect bloom to her withered chest.

"Well, I never!" she exclaimed in tones shrill and shocked. As she turned—some would say it was an accident, others would not be so kind—her bony hip connected with the table, sending pots and blossoms flying. Betty Jameson's gardenia smashed upon the ground, blue ribbon and all.

Miss Watterson didn't look back as she stalked away, shaking her head. After all, she had fifty-two blue ribbons upon her mantle. Mrs Jameson could only have one.

Echoes in the Ashes – April Pereira

(Genre: Drama)

The blackened remains of my manuscript smoldered in the fireplace.

My stomach churned, a wave of bile rising in my throat. I knew this script well—a tale of woe growing louder with each empty bottle and rejection letter. My father was the main act.

My rising talent underscored his failures. I was now the villain. A part of me longed to shrink, just to soften the rage in his eyes. But it was too late. He would burn me down too.

I sifted through the ashes of my work before packing. "I love you, Dad, but this story…it's mine now."

Eel Pearl Jelly Medicine – Misty Mator

(Genre: Action/Adventure)

Buried underwater in my wetsuit, I think of the mythic serpent-slaying Ama diver who rescued her father.

I need to save my son.

Every earthly medicine exhausted, I seek the fabled cure.

I gathered underground fruit of the African Hydnora plant, festering flowers smelling of rot, to preserve the nets.

I picked poison guava from Florida Manchineel trees for bait.

Now I swim down the dark ocean trench, my son's fevered hopes pressing me on.

Finally, the large snaggle-tooth eel looms. I lunge. It's fast. But I'm faster.

"Don't let me wish I'd spent this time *with* him," I pray.

Evil Taught Hannah How to Drive – Trevor Woods

(Genre: Thriller)

Excruciating pain throbs at the base of Hannah's head, slowly pulling her awake into a strange place. It's dark and agonizingly hot. Her sweat-soaked clothes cling to her body—at least, she thinks it's sweat. Wherever she is, the stale, tangible air reeks of old, moldy clothes and motor oil. She squints, focusing her eyes through the darkness. Dim bands of light reveal scattered objects strewn about: Barbie dolls, women's clothes, a coil of rope, and tools whose metallic glints seem oddly familiar. Ah, it's a jack and a four-way wrench—tools she remembers her daddy using on their driveway.

She immediately realizes she can't move as bindings bite into her wrists and ankles. Her mouth is stuffed with rags, secured with layers of tape that leave behind a bitter, gasoline-like taste. The adhesive yanks her skin as she shifts. Positioning herself face-up, pins and needles start dotting her left arm—it's asleep. She feels her body vibrating, and she can hear a light *rumbling* sound.

It dawns on her… she's in the trunk of a car. The car is running, but stationary. *Did someone abduct me?* she thinks, recalling true-crime documentaries she's watched with her mother.

Rushing adrenaline temporarily erases the pain in her body. She begins thrashing as panic sets in, her body contorting and kicking with desperate attempts to free herself. Each movement battles the Texas heat, the compactness of the space, and her bindings, making it nearly impossible to move. As she thrashes, a couple of minutes pass. She becomes exhausted, struggling to inhale through her gag. The heat suffocates her resolve.

Hannah cries.

As despair stifles her determination, the tape on her wrists gives way slightly. Her eyes widen, fueled by a renewed sense of hope. She scissors her hands, working the tape loose, enduring the rawness of her skin. With her right hand free, she jostles the tape around her head, removing the rags. She yanks the hair-mangled tape off her head, ignoring the stinging of hair pulling her scalp.

Seizing the opportunity, she turns to her side and curls into a fetal position to reach her ankles. The tape is slippery with sweat, but she convinces a small edge to give, and she painstakingly unwraps it, again, feeling the burning sensation of ripped skin and hair.

Suddenly, her breathing hitches as she hears the crunching of leaves outside the trunk interrupt her escape efforts.

Hannah freezes… *Who is that?* she thinks.

Every muscle stiffens, rendering her still and silent like a statue. She closes her eyes, attempting to dampen her cries and calm herself. Her heart's beating out of her chest, a resounding thunder reverberating in her ears. She wonders if they can hear it too as she counts the seconds.

Terrified her captor—or captors—will return to find her untied, she listens intently for several minutes. She hears someone milling around, then their fading footsteps trudging through the thick leaves, eventually fading into the distance. *I must be close to the woods,* she thinks.

She waits for the silence to confirm they've left. Her heart rate lowers slightly, and the footsteps disappear.

Hannah gets back to work.

With her bindings removed, she assesses her next challenge: escaping the trunk. She repositions and clears a space from clutter, attempting to kick it open. She violently kicks the trunk several times, but it's futile. Pushing it with her back doesn't yield better results. Realizing brute force isn't working, at least that of a twelve-year-old skinny girl, she collapses, resigning herelf to a deathly fate.

"Momma, Daddy, please find me," she whispers, hoping the ether will carry her words home. She tucks herself into a ball, wanting to disappear. As she pushes herself back, something shifts behind her; she feels a slight, cool breeze caress her neck.

Hannah shivers.

She flips around, discovering that the back seat folds down. Capitalizing on this, she squeezes through the opening, staying low to avoid detection. The fresh, ninety-degree arctic air envelops her entire body and energizes her. Through the car windows, she surveys an isolated road engulfed by forest on both sides. Approximately fifty yards away, she recognizes a man in a red t-shirt and shorts setting up a tent—it's Mr. Miller, her neighbor and girl-scout leader. Anger replaces her fear. "How could you do this?" she mutters.

She fixes her eyes on him as she slithers into the driver's seat, keeping a low profile. Almost over, she catches him glancing in her direction. Hannah quickly ducks down and waits. "Please, please don't notice me," she whispers, sweat forming a wet circle on the seat. Her child-like, bright green eyes slowly crest the top of the frayed vinyl seat to determine if he saw her. They lock eyes. He starts toward the car, shouting, "Hannah, it's not what you think!"

Adrenaline jump-starts her bruise-laden hands into action as she scrambles to start the car. She recalls her parents driving—P for park, D for drive. She shifts to D and slams on the gas. The tires spin, kicking up a wall of rocks that temporarily shield Mr. Miller's advance. Finally, the car lunges forward.

She's lost but continues driving, putting distance between herself and Mr. Miller. After ten minutes on the dirt road, she spots a billboard that says, *Three Sisters Farm*. She turns up a driveway to a red barn adorned with giant hay bales.

Slamming the brakes, she observes a woman in a yellow sundress feeding chickens inside the red barn. Hannah exits both her prison and escape vehicle, running to her and jumping into her arms. The woman, sensing Hannah's distress, holds her tightly, comforting her.

"What happened, honey?" the woman gently prompts, removing strands of hair from Hannah's face.

Hannah tells her story of imprisonment and escape as the woman helps her to her feet. "Let's get to the house and call the police."

On the way, the woman asks, "Who taught you how to drive?"

"Evil taught me how to drive."

Eye For An Eye – Chris Morris

(Genre: Drama)

I fell in love with his voice first. He was shouting at some seagulls for shitting in his hair.

'Hello? Who's there?' My voice came in a quivering whisper.

I heard his delicate footsteps pad towards me, then two soft hands grabbed my shoulders.

'Watch out!'

A cacophony of clamorous clanging sounded at my side. I landed in something sticky.

'Jerks! Look before you throw your trash in the dump! You nearly hit the lady! And *you*, Missus. Whydya not look where you're goin'? Are you *blind*?'

'…Yes.'

A pause. Then: 'Oh. Damn. You got no eyes.'

'That's why I ended up here. Amalie didn't want me anymore.'

More awkward silence.

'Well… at least you got… a nose, I guess.'

I shook my head. If I could have cried, I might have. Then his touch came at my shoulder again, lighter than before.

'You know, I got one to spare.'

'A nose?'

'No, not a nose! Whatdya need *two* noses for? A double-dose of the rotten eggs and fish guts? Here, hold still.'

He pawed at my face. After a moment, he came into view, blurry at first, and then his big, fluffy ears and one black, shiny eye were clear. He had a stitched nose. Just like me.

'There. Should hold for now.'

I fell in love with his kindness second. His selfless, magical, warm kindness.

'I haven't formally introduced myself. Name's Teddy.'

I fell in love with his face third. Shame it was covered in seagull shit.

Flip Your Life – Michał Przywara

(Genre: Comedy)

And just like that, Wally and Barb Flatt's enthusiasm popped, sprinkling dismayed confetti all over, well, the carpet.

"I just don't understand," repeated Mr. Doorworth – the increasingly unprospective buyer of the house – as if there was a shadow of a doubt he had been unclear.

"It's not that we have anything against carpet," Mrs. Doorworth added. "And carpeting the whole house is certainly… an idea. But why would you also carpet the kitchen?"

Wally and Barb looked at each other, no longer grinning. Their hand holding became limp. They'd learned so much at the "Flip your House Flip your Life: How to Leap to the Next Level" interior decorating class they'd taken at the community centre. Their teacher, Chet "the House Guru" Wizard – or was he Chet Guru, "the House Wizard"? – had even said they were his best students: triple A, double plus!

Could they have made a mistake with the carpet? Had they truly carpeted their whole house – and the patio – without ever once stopping to wonder if it was a good idea?

Could Wizard House, "the Chet Guru", have been wrong?

"I mean," said Mrs. Doorworth, "what if somebody knocked over their bottle of wine? That happens in a kitchen."

"A lot," said Mr. Doorworth. "We'd have to tear the

whole thing up. And I don't mean just in the kitchen – the whole house."

"Yeah," said Mrs. Doorworth. "I'm not judging, but I don't know why you went with a different colour in each room."

"Definitely not judging," her husband confirmed. "It's just, we're not carpet people."

Wally sniffed. The carpets had been Barb's idea. But Barb narrowed her eyes because Wally had suggested the colours. They let go of each other's hands.

They'd been so close during the class, so close since they'd taken it. So close, especially compared to how far they'd drifted apart before it. They'd gone to learn how to flip their house, but they'd also learned how to flip their marriage. They'd also learned to laugh again.

And installing the carpets together? Spending all their free time doing back-breaking labour and wasting a fortune in materials, because even measuring twice didn't cut it if you didn't know what you were measuring? That had been a blast. Hadn't it?

They laughed, they talked, they flirted, and they planned. They'd turn this new hobby into a business, and go national, and go on TV. They'd develop carpetosophy as the foremost philosophy of interior design.

Had they made a mistake somewhere along the way?

"You know," Mr. Doorworth said, scratching his chin, "I don't even know the condition of the floors in this house. If I rip up all the carpets… hmm. Lots of work. And at the price you're asking, well, frankly it's an indecent proposal."

The Doorworths guffawed, and then left.

Barb and Wally looked at their carpeted house, and then at each other.

"So," she said. "Divorce?"

"Yup."

For all the Marbles – Robert Burns

(Genre: Romance)

When she was eight, Alice Henderson briefly held the world record for filling her mouth with marbles.

At least, that's how she remembers it.

It was the kind of sweltering summer that went relentlessly on and on; the kind of summer that melted your clothes into your sticky skin, making you wonder if it would ever be cool again.

Alice found Jimmy Riordan kneeling in the dirt under the ancient eucalyptus tree back behind the duck pond, flicking aggies and cat's-eyes in an inscribed circle. The glass orbs were smooth as candy, their icy appearance presenting an odd temptation on such a hot day.

"Watcha doing?" she asked.

The boy looked up. "Playing marbles. What's it look like?" he said, resuming his position. He pulled a few more marbles from his drawstring pouch and sent the shooter clacking into a cluster of glassies.

"Can I play?" Alice studied the toes of her Mary Janes as she traced her own circle in the dirt.

"No," Jimmy said, not bothering to look up. "Girls can't play."

Alice squatted for a closer look. "They sure are pretty."

"Aw, what do you know?"

The girl impetuously snatched a deep emerald taw from the ring and popped it into her mouth.

"Hey!" Jimmy sat back on his heels. "Give it back!"

Alice rolled the silky glass around in her mouth, imagining a green-apple Jolly Rancher as it clicked against her teeth—oddly refreshing. The marble's smoothness contrasted nicely with the texture inside her cheeks, rolling and shifting with each movement of her tongue.

She finally stuck out her tongue, offering the taw to Jimmy on its tip.

"Nope," she laughed, sucking the jewel back into her mouth before the boy could react.

She plucked a blue and white cat's-eye from the ring. Now, two marbles rolled about in her mouth, clinking softly against each other, with a gentle, rhythmic—almost soothing—sound.

"Cut it out!" Jimmy said, although he wasn't really sure he wanted the two marbles back any more. He just wanted the girl to leave him alone. "Listen. I got an idea. You can keep all the marbles you can fit in your mouth," he told Alice, "if you just go away."

The girl nodded with a clack.

Alice studied the dirt ring and popped the ruby shooter into her mouth. Then an aggie.

Then a cat's-eye and another glassy.

Before long, all the marbles were gone from the ring and Alice's cheeks resembled a squirrel's with its mouth full of acorns. Jimmy stared in awe at the elasticity.

Alice proudly displayed her stuffed jowls. "Whuff'sh left in yur powsh?" she managed to get out.

Jimmy Riordan held out his pouch and fell in love.

133

Fortified – Misty Mator

(Genre: Drama)

A heavyhearted visit to Grandfather's property.

The wooden rungs are long gone, but the dumbwaiter is still there. The overgrown grass itches the back of my knees, and I can nearly hear the echo of Grandpa's voice.

"You just pull on this here rope, and you can haul up books, vittles, whatever you want up to your tree fort."

"Vittles?"

"Grandma's cookies."

The memory stirs a familiar longing, an aching in my chest. The faded blue tree fort recalls stories told by flashlight, a sweet to go with every scrape, the smell of Old Spice aftershave mingled with drying lavender in the kitchen.

I know he wouldn't be mad. He'd say selling this old place is the "right smart" thing to do. When he died, I went about fixing all the problems a death leaves: calling insurance companies, consolidating investments, contacting utilities, the like. I've done anything and everything – except selling the house with this old tree fort.

I've been holding onto this property, my last vestige of childhood, as if holding onto it could take me back. Back to him.

I'm old enough now to know he didn't actually have all the answers. But when he didn't have an answer, he'd find a way to share a laugh with me. I miss that.

I stand under the barren oak branches, staring up at the old tree fort. I zip my hoodie up against the autumn wind. Grandpa always thought I "looked the fool" the way I wear shorts year-round; it always cracked him up.

God, how I crave to hear his laugh, just one more time.

I know it's stupid, but I test my weight on the oversized dumbwaiter. Despite its complaints, the rusty wheel turns as I pull myself up into the tree. This was Grandpa's favorite way into our hideout.

"No ruminatin' in the tree fort."

It was Grandpa's rule. It meant that he left whatever worries he was wrestling with down on the grass and just focused on "livin' in the tree fort world" with me.

So I stop thinking about the cost of my daughter's surgery, taxes, selling this place.

I breathe in the smell of old wood and think about slip knots, secret passwords, Redwall novels read aloud.

I think about learning chess, Grandpa never letting me win, and him chuckling every time I lost. I remember he laughed the loudest when I finally won, relishing the real win with me.

I remember stories, songs, and so many plates of Grandma's vittles.

I let all the memories wash over me, all the *good* I had been given in this place, all the love one old man could muster for an only grandchild to last that child a lifetime.

Sunlight dappling down on my face, I realize I can finally let this old fort he built go. Because what he built *lives in me.*

I can imagine him chortling, "Took ya' long enough, sitting in them fool shorts." Through my overdue tears, I begin to laugh.

It sounds just like Grandpa's.

Go Find Your Sunshine – Russell Mickler

(Genre: Romantic Comedy)

A doorless Jeep Wrangler rolled up to the coffee station's plexiglass service window.

Wren squeezed the nail glue onto one of her red acrylics and pressed it against her middle finger. "You again?"

"Why not? Coffee's good, service, too," the driver said, resting their foot on the fender flare to glance behind them. "Even if I'm the only one here."

"Nobody but you wants coffee on a hot day, honey. It's Troy, right?"

"Trei," they replied. Trei had spiky black hair cropped short and wore a t-shirt, cargo shorts, and Mephistos. Their eyes tracked downward, devouring Wren's figure behind their mirrored sunglasses. "And that's the third time now, honey."

Dressed in a string bikini, Wren approached the window. "Sorry. Too many customers, but it's the orders I remember. Faces."

Trei tipped their chin. "Yeah? You like my face?"

"Venti, half-caf, extra-shot, caramel macchiato. Almond milk. 160-degrees. Cinnamon."

Trei added, "With a drizzle of white chocolate."

"Right," Wren said. "A sweet tooth."

"Teeth ain't the only thing sweet on me, baby."

Wren playfully regarded Trei as she brought the espresso

machine to temperature. "No doubt. Got big plans today?"

Trei gestured to the racked surfboard above their head. "Huntington, south pier. Was thinkin' of hitting the waves for a few hours, then heading back home before rush hour."

Wren purged the espresso maker, releasing pressurized steam and wiping the excess water with a cloth. "Hmm. That typhoon in the Philippines?"

"Six-footers, they're sayin'," Trei replied, stretching, running a hand down the back of their neck. Trei stared longingly at Wren's curves. "Best we've had in a while."

"So you don't work then?" Wren asked, pouring the almond milk into the frothing pitcher.

Trei recoiled. "I work."

"You some surfy-beach bum?"

"I'm in real estate—"

"Independently wealthy, maybe?" Wren interjected, dipping the steam wand into the pitcher with a squelch. "I can tell. Mommy and Daddy mail you a stipend from Iceland, huh?"

"Guilt payments," Trei admitted. "A few grand, but it barely pays the rent."

Wren smacked the portafilter, sending a clump of wet grounds into the sink.

"They bolted when I was seventeen. Gave me three hundred bucks and left me on Sunset Boulevard. My dad? He even said, 'Hasta la vista' as he drove off."

"Jerk!"

Trei shrugged. "It was the nineties."

"Where'd you go after that?"

"I lived in a shipping container for a while."

Wren tsked. "Rough."

Trei raised their eyebrows; Wren's tanned body reflected in their shades. "Nah. The experience made me appreciate what little I had. Besides, I met this homeless guy from Tanzania. Traded sex for him to teach me how to hunt rats."

Wren sneered. "Gross!"

"They're not so bad fried, with catsup."

"You know, we do have a pay-what-you-can program we offer to all our drive-thru millionaires."

Trei sniggered and paused before wistfully glancing out the windshield. "They didn't care for who I was. So they left. Whatever."

"Shitty, selfish behavior," Wren said as she tamped the coffee and inserted the portafilter into the group head. "But some of us gotta work, honey."

"Probably not too much with an ass like that. Wish I could reach out and—"

"Uh-huh, that's what the plexiglass is for," Wren smirked, arching her back to accentuate her generous posterior. She hit the steam valve; a stream of tar-black liquid extruded into the shot glass. The milk frothed.

Trei squirmed in the driver's seat. "How about you? Why do … this?"

Wren prepared Trei's extra shot. "I used to be an insurance adjuster."

Trei rolled their eyes. "Bullshit."

"Policies. Assessments. Settlements. Four years I'll never get back."

"Hard to imagine," Trei mused.

"Ask me about your Wrangler."

Trei laughed. "Okay, but why bikini coffee?"

"I used to live in Portland. The sun would rise after I got to work and set before I left. And after nine hours, I only wanted to sleep."

"Harsh."

Wren locked the portafilter. "Ever done that? Live out your life in the dark?"

"Nope."

Wren squinted into the sunlight streaming through the window. "Here, doing this, I get all the sun I want."

Trei relaxed against the headrest. "Don't you get tired of it, though?"

"What? Sun?"

"No, the ogling."

Wren snorted, curving her pour to leave a macchia mark on top of the espresso. "Well, bless your heart for thinking it all stops when I step outside this box. I might as well get paid for it, shouldn't I?"

"You could dance? Great tips. You could work less and play more. Some would love to see you wrapped around a pole."

Wren winked. "Poles aren't my thing, sugar."

Trei exhaled, flattening the lines of their shorts. "So what brought you to L.A.?"

"Sex work," Wren sighed, drizzling sticky chocolate ropes over the top of Trei's drink. "The raunchy, kinky stuff, too."

"Guess that didn't pan out?"

Wren licked her fingertips free of syrup. "No, but it led me to what I wanted."

Trei clenched the steering wheel. "And what was that?"

Coming around the counter, Wren's hips rolled as she leaned through the window to hand Trei their drink.

"A compassionate boi," she grinned, "who cares more about living their life than making money."

Trei, transfixed, gripped the cup even though it scalded their hands. Sweat beaded on their forehead.

"Careful," she breathed, closing on Trei. "Contents are hot."

Trei's tongue traced her glossy lips when they kissed.

Gently pulling away, Wren batted her sultry brown eyes. "I get off at four."

Trei gulped.

"And you'd better be home when I get there," Wren scolded. "Don't be stupid."

"I won't be stupid," Trei whispered, averting their eyes.

"Be especially not stupid today. There'll be big waves."

Trei chortled. "I will. Chinese okay?"

"I'm down. Better than rats again."

Placing the drink into the cup holder, Trei disabled the brake and put the Jeep into gear. "Gods, I love you."

"And I adore you," Wren replied, caressing Trei's smooth jawline as an irritated customer behind them impatiently honked their horn.

Halloween Decorations – Chris Morris

(Genre: Horror)

I hate Halloween. But at least it's the one night of the year I can get away with such extreme décor.

I hang them.

Two more teenagers appear. They compliment my grinning pumpkin decorations. Ugh. A werewolf and a vampire. How irritating.

A thud at the door.

Slam.

I grab my hammer. Flash a smile back at my pumpkins. Next to them, a ghostly face wails.

A little adjustment. Now it'll stop moving so much.

Rope. That'll do the trick. Hold the squirmy thing in place.

Another trick-or-treater. Wearing a white ghost mask.

I invite him in.

Best read upwards.

Happy Father's Day, Darling – Trevor Woods

(Genre: Drama)

Lena snuck out of bed early before her kids livened the house with chaotic bantering and begging for pancakes—Saturday morning pancakes were a Foster family tradition. She had approximately one hour to do several hours' worth of chores before the kids got up—an impossible task.

"Good morning, honey," Lena's mother greeted as she poured a steaming, hot cup of hazelnut coffee, Lena's favorite. She slogged to the kitchen, wiping the sleep and exhaustion from her eyes, offering one last yawn before the day started. Being a devoted mother of four was all-consuming, so her mother's visits were much-needed reprieves. But she wasn't just a mother of four, she was a tutor, taxi-driver, maid, cook, and everything in-between.

Having her favorite coffee ready was just the morale-boost Lena needed. She forced a smile as she walked through the hazelnut aroma hovering in the kitchen. *Sometimes the best morning greeting is Colombian coffee beans, not words,* Lena thought.

"Good morning, Mom," she answered, planting a kiss on her cheek.

Lena cherished her mother's visits while Steve was away fighting his wars. Her mom provided her with rare "me" time, as she explained to the kids. She would visit the local Barnes & Noble, sip her caramel macchiato, meditate, and read. Of course, she also ran errands, but she didn't mind—it allowed her to accomplish tasks she otherwise wouldn't have had time for.

This would be the fourth consecutive Father's Day Steve had been gone.

"Is Steve going to call today?" asked Lena's mother.

"He usually does." Her non-committal answer was truer than a yes or no because he *usually* did call. But there was no way of knowing if he was safe enough to call, near a phone, or even alive.

That's what made raising four kids alone worse—the gnawing uncertainty of her husband's safety in faraway battlefields, in countries she couldn't pronounce. She no longer knew what he was fighting for and didn't care anymore.

She dreaded incoming calls while he was away, especially when the caller ID failed. For her, a harmless call was extremely unsettling; the initial feeling of her heart dropping into her stomach, the nerve-racking initial conversation trying to decipher the context, and the fleeting relief that it was just a telemarketer. If she were to ever meet a telemarketer, it would take her great restraint to not give them a piece of her mind.

Her mother took one last sip of her coffee and stood up. "What do you need help with, honey?"

"If you could start the laundry, that would be fantastic," Lena suggested as she started unloading the dishwasher.

Lena's phone rang. Her heart stopped as she ran to answer it.

"Hello?"

"Hi, Lena. It's Steve. I just wanted to call to wish you a Happy Father's Day, darling."

Lena smiled as her eyes started to well.

As tears began falling down her cheeks, she felt relieved to hear her husband's voice. Her relief also included tears of deep gratitude for Steve, who appreciated her tireless commitment to their family, filling his role as father while he was gone.

Have a Seat Misery – Beth Connor

(Genre: Horror)

City streets morph into rolling hills, rushing by in a blur of misty silhouettes. A man of middling years gazes out the grime-streaked train window, his piercing blue eyes tracking the changing scene. Moonlight strikes the panes, turning their dullness to opal and silver. He reaches out to brush a fingertip across a woman's arm.

Her eyes, wide and unblinking, betray a deep-seated dread as she stands beside him. She draws a tasseled shawl tight around her slouched shoulders.

"Have a seat. Put your feet up," he says.

Ice cubes in the tumbler clink together as the man stirs his whiskey. He peels his eyes away from the window and glances at the woman. She slips into a chair across from him, unfolding a pristine white napkin. She runs a tongue over pale lips, her mouth turning up in a smile that does not meet her eyes. As she tilts her head, she regards the man.

"Don't cry at me, thinking I kept you away for too long. To me, you have never been gone," he continues. Dingy windows rattle as the train passes over a wooden bridge, creaks and clatters filling the silence.

"Your hands are shaking. Let me light that for you," the man says, his voice dripping with condescension as he plucks the cigarette from the woman's slender fingers. He strikes a match and watches as a tiny flicker of light ignites.

He inserts the cigarette into an intricate jade holder and presses it to the woman's lips. She inhales. Her chest expands, then she exhales a small stream of smoke. "Oh, how I've missed you," he says, perhaps to the woman, but more likely to the alcohol. He balances the cigarette holder on a crystal ashtray and tries to brush away the dark smudge of exhaustion underneath the woman's eyes.

Her chest rises and falls; aside from that, she is still. The dark fog surrounding her seems to expand, tendrils clawing and reaching for the man. "You would be nothing without me." He is serious for a moment, then melts into a half smile. "But of everyone, you are the one I love most."

Three times the train whistles and wails like the sorrowful cry of a bean sídhe, foretelling and forlorn. The man scans the empty dining car before turning back to the woman. "It won't be long now."

She sighs, disregarding him, and turns to watch out the window. He raises an eyebrow but says nothing before following her gaze. Dark storm clouds have rolled in, releasing their despair in the form of fat droplets onto a small family standing on the platform. The train squeals as it slides into the station.

"We've got damage to do," he states and pushes a plate at the woman. "Best have something to eat." His face is all angles now, sinister and cruel. She pushes the food around with a silver fork.

The family boards: a mother, a father, and a child not much older than ten. They are always so innocent at the start of a journey. It won't be long before that changes.

The man narrows his eyes as he observes the boy, sensing something off about him—an unsettling aura flickering like a shadow at the edge of the lamplight. When their eyes meet, it feels as though the air between them thickens, a palpable tension tightening its grip. The boy smiles, but there is something in his gaze, a knowingness that makes the man's skin prickle.

Uneasiness grips the woman as she watches. Her fingers twitch. He weaves his way through the tables with an unnerving grace, as if floating rather than walking. Her breath quickens, and a thin line of perspiration forms on her upper lip.

The boy approaches the man and woman. He knows what they are hiding, and he knows what they are here for. But they do not know what he is here for. "'Scuse me, sir, may I sit here with you? My ma and da have gone to sleep. It is night, and I am bored and lonely."

The man curls his lips up in a sneer and pulls out a chair, inviting the child to have a seat. "Of course, young man. What parents would be so cruel as to leave their child unattended on such a dark and stormy eve?"

With no answer, the boy slides into the oversized chair. The woman is silent. She sinks into herself, chewing on her lip. There is nothing to see out the window anymore. Just inky darkness threatening to swallow them whole. However, both the man and the woman continue to stare outside.

"I've always loved train rides," the boy says with a shy smile that makes his eyes crinkle. "Did you know if the water in the steam engine's boiler gets too low, the entire engine can explode?"

"Best hope the engineer is paying attention," the man says. "Where did you say your parents were sitting?"

The boy doesn't notice the man's words, sharp as a knife's

edge. Time seems to slow, dark and sticky like molasses. The woman balls her fists, nails leaving tiny half-moons in her palms, and the lights in the dining car dim, letting the shadows feast on the light.

"It looks like we are almost at the end of the line," the boy states, and the man breaks into a peal of maniacal laughter.

"That's where you are wrong. This route has no terminus." Blue eyes turn cold. "Just an endless loop of misery and despair."

"I wasn't talking about the train."

It is already too late when the man finally looks into the boy's eyes. Deep pools darker than the blackest night. Empty sockets, drinking him in.

"Who are you?"

The boy regards him for the briefest of moments before answering. "I am nothing," he says as the dark overtakes them all. "I am the end."

Heart of Stone, Wings of Hope – April Pereira

(Genre: Fairy Tale)

In the heart of the mountain, where hope withered, dwelt Elara. Kestrel the fox saw her plight and whispered promises of freedom.

One day, Kestrel placed a dozen eggs before her, a gleam in his eye.

Elara frowned, her thoughts flashing back to the day of her imprisonment: a gaunt figure with desperate eyes pleading for sustenance. Sneering, she had clutched her basket of eggs tighter and walked past.

"Eggs? That's how I got into this mess!"

"These eggs," Kestrel said, "hold the power to break free."

Setting aside her gnawing self-doubt and despair, Elara accepted the fox's eggs.

Weeks passed as she tended the eggs, her heart growing fonder for her charges each day. She cradled them, whispering encouragement.

The eggs hatched to reveal tiny creatures of earth and sky, and as the last cracked, the mountain shuddered, opening a fissure in the stone. Sunlight flooded the chamber, and Elara followed the hatchlings out. Stepping into the light, Elara caught her breath. There stood the beggar, laughter dancing in his eyes. She watched him transform first into Kestrel, then into Turms, the trickster.

"You were a prisoner of your selfishness, Elara," Turms declared. "True freedom comes from within."

Shame weighed on Elara's shoulders but amidst it, hope ignited. Descending the mountain path, gravel crunching beneath her feet, she found a baby bird struggling on the ground. Gently, she picked it up, its tiny heart fluttering against her palm. She carefully placed it back in its nest and continued home.

Heart of the Sky – April Pereira

(Genre: Fantasy)

In a cloud-kissed town perched at the lip of the sky lived a wisp of a girl named Lila. While most her age spent their days tending cloud-cows or weaving dreams into tapestries, Lila spent hours gazing at the turbid skies, her mind adrift in whispered legends of colossal beasts whose mournful songs guided lost sailors to safe harbor. Some dismissed the stories as old wives' tales, but Lila clung to them, her heart a compass pointed towards the fabled aurora borealis.

One night, as the sky blazed with emerald fire, Lila stood frozen, breathless, as an impossible sight broke through the ethereal canvas—a magnificent whale breaching the clouds, towing a rickety contraption of weathered wood and gleaming brass. Brimming with excitement and curiosity, Lila hurriedly prepared her airship—a marvel of mismatched parts and fizzy pop—and set sail in pursuit of the magnificent whale.

***

After countless nights of chasing stardust, Lila came upon the whale. On the weathered deck of the tethered boat stood a man. He introduced himself as Captain Silas and explained his noble quest.

"The Heart of the Skies," he said, "is more than a gem. It's the key to restoring harmony. If it isn't renewed with the whale's song, storm giants will overtake the skies."

Lila, her eyes wide with wonder, nodded. "I want to help."

Thus began an unlikely alliance—a wide-eyed dreamer,

a seasoned captain, and a celestial behemoth. They battled storms that raged with the fury of a thousand disgruntled sky-gnomes, navigated treacherous cloud mazes, and faced down ancient guardians with voices like thunder. Through it all, Lila learned. Captain Silas, with his unwavering optimism, taught her the value of perseverance. With its calming presence and deep connection to the sky, the whale showed her the power of hope.

***

They reached the peak of the world, where the sky kissed the stars. Storm giants, eager to keep the crew from their destination, called forth a tempest, its fury a living, breathing entity. Lightning cracked like whiplash, and the wind howled like a wounded beast. Their rickety vessel shuddered and threatened to splinter. Lila clung to the railing, knuckles white, as the whale, its usually calm eyes filled with urgency, dove beneath them. Then, it rose, its colossal body a shield against the storm's onslaught. Yet, the vessel creaked and groaned, timbers straining under the storm's relentless assault. A single, decisive blow could shatter their dreams.

As they pushed through the storm, they found the Heart of the Skies in a nest of stardust and clouds pulsating with an ethereal glow. The gem responded as the whale sang its haunting melody, sending a wave of pure harmony through the celestial expanse. Lila felt peace wash over her, the once-discolored clouds blooming with vibrant hues.

Their mission complete, the whale dipped its head in farewell, its song echoing through the newly serene sky. Content with the restored balance, Captain Silas and Lila set sail on his ramshackle boat, forever chasing the horizon.

Henry Hewitt – Chris Morris

(Genre: Comedy)

This is the tale of Henry Hewitt

Who when he ate his lunch would say: 'Ah, screw it!

'As my chomping teeth make my food all broken

'I'll keep my mouth all wide and open!'

For that was the way of Henry Hewitt

When he stuffed food in his mouth and began to chew it

His mouth would water and his lips would smack

With his sickly guzzling he wouldn't hold back.

He'd take bigger bites than was wise to do

And then he would sweat and his hands would shake too

He'd whimper and groan as though in distress

His work shirt was ruined, his mouth was a mess.

With a smirk he'd continue, would Henry Hewitt

Like the back of his hand he bloody well knew it

His colleagues would sit with fingers in ears

Lunch break was top on their list of deep fears.

And when he was done, the torture didn't end

He'd lick his fingers end to end

Then with a belch and a groan he would stretch his arms wide

And his gaseous fumes weren't kept on the inside.

But soon there came a plot against Hewitt

His colleagues had chuckled at the thought they would do it

His lunch was unguarded in a box in the fridge

So Henry's co-workers altered it a smidge.

Brenda kept watch while David unbottled

A nasty concoction all lumpy and mottled

And when Brenda returned and said, 'He's coming!'

The pair dashed to their seats and their hearts were drumming.

Out of the fridge came a box marked "Hewitt"

He missed the chilli sauce that was laced all through it

And he slurped and he guzzled with his mouth wide open

Until the heat of the sauce was finally awoken.

Sweat poured from his brow and tears ran from his eye

He said: 'Jesus Christ, I think I might die!'

He roared louder than the chords of the King's College choir.

Smoke billowed from a tongue enveloped in fire.

But the following day, his colleagues felt sad

Perhaps their revenge was disproportionately bad

But Henry Hewitt was met with more laughter

When they learned of his rear-end pain the morning after.

Hope Blossoms – April Pereira

(Genre: Drama)

Cherry blossoms, a riot of pink, swirled around Anna and David. The breeze a soft melody after the cacophony of the infusion pumps. David's rhythmic typing a soothing counterpoint. Anna's fingers hovered over her keyboard, the once vibrant instrument silenced by the poisons that defined her last two years. David's hand, a warm anchor, found hers. A soft half-smile touched his lips in silent understanding. A spark ignited in Anna's eyes. Her fingers flew, each keystroke a testament to their love and her returning voice. "The salty spray kissed Isla's lips, whispering promises of adventure."

Hot Chocolate – Jon Casper

(Genre: Sci-Fi)

Anastasia huddled beside her mother, eyes reflecting the faint glow of the Indigo Bloom on distant hills. "Will it hurt, Mommy?"

Delara adjusted the focus on her telescope. "They say it's like going to sleep." The white lie left a foul aftertaste as another earthward blue streak scratched the horizon, flared brighter than lightning, then blinked out.

The girl's voice was soft as the southern breeze. "It's pretty."

Delara tightened the blanket around their shoulders in the cool spring night, choking back a sob.

Let her believe.

#

Colonel Anton slapped the conference table. "We're someone's goddamn *garbage dump*?"

Dr. Delara Maldonado stifled a flinch, defying the officer's intimidation tactics. "To be blunt, yes. The organism presents taxonomically as a fungus, but its biology is singular. The megaton objects, apparently extra-dimensional in origin, incinerate in the atmosphere. Only the spores survive, scattering through the troposphere and falling with the rain."

"You mean extra-terrestrial."

"No, from another *dimension*. Whoever's doing the refuse transferrence took *out of sight, out of mind* one step further:

out of *existence*. It comes from Earth, but in a universe where evolution divaricated into something unrecognizable to us. Their planet is slightly out of phase with our orbit, too, thus the parcels present as meteors."

The colonel paced the length of the table. "What about N95?"

Delara frowned. "We have yet to identify effective PPE. At just .05 microns, the Indigo Bloom spores slip past even our most advanced filtration systems. The one blessing, to use the word generously, is how fast it kills. But for those five minutes …"

The colonel's face paled as he dropped into a chair. "So, that's it? We kiss our asses goodbye?"

"We're out of options, Colonel. Make peace with that irrefutable fact and whatever god you worship."

#

Anastasia shivered while peering through the telescope, her tongue jutting over her lips like it always did when she was enthralled.

Delara's little girl wouldn't have long to wait for another spectacle of light. Evidently, the inter-dimensional disposal business was booming. The bolide bombardment had increased tenfold in the week since the doctor had given her expert testimony before top brass at Homeland Security.

Colonel Anton had been on the news that morning, having made a twelve gauge exit in the shed behind his suburban home.

"You look cold, Ana." Delara pressed a thermos into her daughter's cool fingers as sapphire mycelium slithered beneath the green grass. "This'll keep you warm."

"Thanks, Mommy." The girl drank her fill before wiping away a chocolate mustache. "What about you?"

Delara smoothed her daughter's hair, imagining the woman she would never become, dreaming of all she might have achieved, envisioning the grandchildren who might have listened to her stories about the universe.

There's no one I'd rather share this with.

Delara finished the thermos of hot chocolate while Anastasia *oohed* and *aahed* into the telescope at the blue meteor shower. The sedatives would spare them from the worst.

Cocoa had never tasted as sweet nor as bitter.

Human Curiosities – Deidra Whitt Lovegren

(Genre: Drama)

"Tell me about Grandfather," I suggest, clipping a lavalier mic onto Éva's red floral blouse. It matches her hair, her lipstick, and her high heels prominently placed on the wheelchair's footrest.

"Vhy him? Your grandfather vas not interesting man."

"Please, Babka. It's for posterity. We need to record your stories."

Frowning, she pulls out a cigarette from a tarnished silver case. After lighting it like a silent film star, she inhales deeply. Through a plume of blue smoke, she says, "Do not call me Babka. Always I am Éva."

I suppress a smile while adjusting the levels to capture her every word.

"You pass ashtray, yes?"

I do. She artfully flicks an inch of embers into it.

"Vhat to say on recording?"

"Tell me how you lost your eye."

Her right hand steals up to feel her black eye patch. It's festooned with rhinestones. "Oh, zis. From days with Barnum and Bailey. Gift from tightrope walker named František — as useless vith a long pole as vith his short von." She laughs, lights another cigarette. "It vas accident. A lovers' quarrel." She waves off the memory.

"Did you love František?"

"Hard to remember. So many years have flown by. Like birds in winter." She pauses, deep in thought. She runs her fingers through her thinning curls, reaffixing a jeweled hairpin.

"How long did you work for the circus?" I prompt her.

"Not long. Vith only von eye, no more trapeze. No more acrobatics." She shrugs. "I vas sent to work vith freak show."

I drop my coffee cup. Éva looks pleased with herself as I dab cold brown splotches off the table with paper napkins. "You worked *where*?"

She purses her lips, then speaks slowly. "I tended circus freaks." She points her cigarette at me like a dagger. "It is vhere I learned to nurse. Before war. Before I vas saboteur for Czech Resistance. But zat is another story."

"You were a nurse for Barnum and Bailey's sideshow?"

"Yes."

"The Greatest Show on Earth?"

"Of course, yes. I rubbed hunched backs, wrapped clubbed feet, stretched wry necks. I treated fire-eaters' burns and removed lice from bearded lady. All patients fell in love vith me, so I had to nurse broken hearts, too." She gives me an impish grin, her green eye undimmed by time.

"Did you ever reciprocate anyone's feelings?"

She leans forward. "Von time only. Good looking man. Patient who could recite 'Vltava' by heart — ah, he could take blue from sky!"

"What happened to him?"

"His conjoined twin disliked me. He kept us awake all

night complaining.”

My eyebrows raise as my jaw drops.

“Romance vas brief. Besides, there vas charming craftsman at circus. He could make anything. He vas carpenter, metalworker, glassblower…”

“He sounds *useful*,” I say.

“After first date, he presented me with first glass eye. The iris color matched *perfectly*. So I married him.”

“Hold on, Éva,” I interrupt. “Grandfather wasn’t a glassblower. He was an accountant.”

Éva shrugs, waving the smoke away. “Vell, then. Never mind.”

I Have Never Tasted Wine – thomas iannucci

(Genre: Comtemplative)

I have never tasted wine,

As bitter as my wasted time,

And I have never met a thief,

Who stole as much from me as sleep,

You see for me the steady beat,

Of time propels my heavy feet,

To go as far as I can bear,

Though I know neither why nor where,

So ever on my story goes,

And how it ends I do not know,

Except for this, the final line:

In a land of wasted time,

I have not

wasted

mine.

I'm Yours – Alexis Araneta

(Genre: Romance)

The day I first saw you and stuck a needle in your shrapnel-damaged arm, you barely managed to whisper "I'm yours" through the layers of blood-stained gauze wrapped around your head. You tried to prop yourself and move to the edge of your rickety metal cot to move closer to me. As I walked away to tend to other battered bodies, your hazel eyes burnt into my heart, making it yours.

The day you hung up your camouflage uniform for the last time, you asked me "I'm yours?" as you held a bouquet of tulips out to me. You nervously put one foot in front of the other, your pacing reverberating in the wooden floor of the dance hall, to move even closer to me. As I ran into your outstretched arms, I nodded to you and let my bow lips touch your cheek, making them yours.

The day I walked down the aisle in a lacy, white gown and a gossamer veil, you tearfully mouthed out "I'm yours" when I finally reached you. You stepped forward, took my delicate hands in yours and pressed them to your soft lips to move closer to me. As I watched you beam at me through the fabric covering my face, I tenderly declared "I do", making me yours.

The day I wailed as contractions ripped through my body like an earthquake, you cooed "I'm yours" as you rubbed my back in small, deep circles. You grabbed a broken, unstable chair and set it next to my bed to move closer to me. As they placed the little girl with your aquiline nose and my ebony hair in your arms, you sobbed, making the mission of protecting her and cherishing her yours.

The days I asked you to open a tight-lipped jar, you would simply reply "I'm yours" before unscrewing the unyielding lid. The day I walked across a stage in a full-length black robe with tails on the sleeves, you bellowed out "I'm yours" as I received my diploma. The day our youngest walked out the door, suitcases in hand, you sighed "I'm yours" in my ear as you held me and I sobbed on your shirt. Each time, you moved a little closer to my heart.

So, every day, as your memory grows thinner than the battlefield gauze when we first met, I can only answer "I'm yours" whenever you ask me who I am. As I watch your hazel eyes light up yet again, I think of your smile through my gossamer veil all those years ago and thank the heavens that my life is yours.

Ink – Kay Northbridge

(Genre: Horror)

Birmingham, England, 1872

The flow from the nib of my pen is smooth on any surface. The barrel sits perfectly in my fingers and the silver band around the ivory-white grip catches the lamp light in such a delightful way. I've not needed any other writing tool since I made this, of real bone. Though my wife, my biggest critic, is such a traditionalist. She argues, *of course*, that I should write in black ink, as is the modern convention. Each time she hints, I simply say:

"Don't read it, if it displeases you."

I dip, write, pause, and blot in careful sequence, hour after hour, supported by my father's walnut desk. The rhythm is comforting and, though it takes time for my letters to stain, I am making good progress on my subject.

Ah, my subject. The beauty of the young women from the back-to-back terraces. They unwittingly claw at my senses, from their flowing locks to the smoky scent of their clothing. Everything about them grabs my attention. To capture that essence, that perfect being, is my wish. I made time and prepared my own materials, having married a girl from their number. I am on the cusp of achieving my deepest want.

The golden silence is broken by a cough and a thud on the floor. The guttural whining starts again. The sleeping draft is wearing off. My wife's timing is perfect. I am reaching the final line of my poem and I scribe the last word with a flourish. I pull myself up from the desk and lift my work in my hands. The subtle texture of the yellow-pink page is pleasing to my fingertips.

With care I approach her, step by gentle step. She shudders in the shadows as if cold, but the log fire warms the air.

I hold up the completed work in front of my face, to show to her deep brown eyes. Written in pleasing cursive over the smoothly shaven skin, my words are the epitome of eloquence. I've left the crimson rose tattoo intact at the top of the piece. It sets off the red lettering and marks the personal nature of her own contribution to the work.

Lowering the skin allows me to examine my companion as her body writhes over the straw bedding, pulling herself along with desperate hands, dragging her torso and the oozing stumps of her thighs.

"There's so much blood," she says, pointing at my work.

I only have one thing to say to her as I turn away, hurt again by her disapproval of my choice of ink.

"Don't read it, if it displeases you."

Journey into Love and Magic – Míriam Toyama

(Genre: Fantasy)

"Listen to me, Eloise! I'm here too." That was the first thing Delila said. And because her inner voice wouldn't shut up, Eloise decided to name her: Delila. Delila felt welcomed and shared her every thought.

"Eloooiiiiise! Let's do something else, have a different job, leave the traveling circus."

"The circus protects us; I know it's hard at first, but it connects us to magic."

"Magic has left this world."

"True, but there are small pieces of it, little shining threads of magic. All of them connected to love. There's magic when you care for someone. When amazing things come into existence just because you love what you do, or you love whom you are doing it to."

"What're you doing? Is it because you love me?"

"I'm making a human, a companion."

"What? How?"

"What makes a human? Bits and bobs, pieces of dreams, slices of memories. Does he really need a beating heart and a speaking mouth? Maybe not; maybe just an aching soul is enough."

"A soul?"

"They're pretty common. Also, we had one in storage," Eloise says, showing a little jar with a shining thing inside.

"No… you can't bring him back! He lied to us!"

"He loved us once; he can do it again."

"He used us! Never loved us! There are so many people in the world! You don't need to make one!"

"I've tried making friends and finding lovers. But they always die, always leave!"

"Humans are feeble, temporary! Why now?"

"Now I know how. I just have to give him something of mine: you!"

"What? Is this revenge? Who are you punishing? Him? Us? Me? Is it because we believed in him? He didn't stay the first time!"

"He'll stay! I'll make him mine! He'll have no eyes, will see no other. He'll have legs, but won't be able to run. And you'll be there, to tame him!"

"I don't want to! We've outlived most of our people, but you have me! And I have you! You are my anchor; you guide me through this existence. Who am I to you?"

"You are part of me and I am part of you. But I'm tired!"

"It's their nature! One day we'll be gone too! And no one will remember us because we stopped living, stopped loving!"

"It's too tiring! To love and lose, start all over again!"

"It's what makes it worth it! Loving and missing… Eloise, let him go."

"Is it? Is it the suffering that makes it worthwhile?"

"Not the suffering. Suffering, sadness, all that, it comes

from missing their smile, hearing their voices in the wind. You know this. You are smarter than me."

"Can we? Can we really still love and be loved? Can we make our way back into the world?"

"I bet we can. I bet it's going to be the best thing we do this century, to love and laugh again," she said as Eloise opened the little jar, and both watched as the little light dispersed into the sky.

Last Train Out – Robert Burns

(Genre: Drama)

I struggled to the platform at Gare du Nord, leather valise under each arm. The incessant rat-a-tat-tat of raindrops drumming on tin roof drowned out the chaos of the throng clamoring to board the train.

There he is.

"Where is she?" Mr. Richard pleaded.

"Gone. Checked out." I handed him the note.

He stared through her words bleeding in the droplets off the brim of his fedora.

"Time to go, Sir."

Mr. Richard climbed the car step behind me and slumped against the doorway, eyes vacant. He tossed the crumpled paper to the railbed as the train lurched forward.

Leap of Faith – Suma Jayachandar

(Genre: Drama)

I pop a peanut-sized yellow ball followed by a green one. And gag.

Turmeric and neem. One for the heart and another for the gut—as Grandma puts it. Wise as ever. She knows exactly what I need. Always has.

The morning sun floods the kitchen. The window frames her shadow on the red oxide floor. I am in a safe space. She turns and winks.

"Ragi roti coming up in ten minutes."

"Let me help you with chutney." I saunter towards the blender.

"No, Putti. You are tired," she says. My mouth quivers, and she adds, "From your journey."

Three and a half hours on a train from Udupi to Goa isn't something a nineteen-year-old gets tired from. And Grandma is no fool.

The rotis served with coconut chutney taste divine after four months of hostel food. It makes me forget for a moment Ma and Pa must be anxious by now.

If only I had the sense to bottle up my emotions! I poked a hornet's nest on the last call.

"Ma, I'm not happy here."

"…Nobody goes to an engineering college to be happy! Everyone has to slog to make it in their lives. Look at your Pa and look at me. Have you ever seen us lazing around?"

"I'm not lazing around! I just don't like it!!"

"Listen, Mona. We discussed it at length before you joined the college. The deal was—you pass with a degree certificate in your hand and then do whatever you want."

"Ma, I tried. But I can't…I want to come home."

"And do what? Click photos and make reels? Do you think you are Rancho from 3 Idiots?"

"What?"

"…"

"Ma, I want to create content. I don't want to become an engineer."

"All the best for your exams starting tomorrow. Good night."

I did write my exams all right. But I was in no mood to go home to my parents for my term break. And when I arrived at Grandma's place last evening, unannounced, she didn't bat an eyelid. Just enveloped me in her warmth.

Grandma and Ma. Mother and daughter. How could they be so different?

It's well past lunchtime when I get up from my siesta.

I take my backpack, tell Grandma I'm going to the beach, and head out.

The warm yielding sand and blue crashing waves ply out my anguish. The gentle breeze peels and carries it away. The setting sun brings the clarity I craved.

At dinner, over rice and chicken xacuti, I ask, "Grandma, you always look so happy and content. Don't you have any regrets?"

She looks up, pauses, and whispers, "Not really…maybe just one thing…I wish I hadn't dropped out of school."

I nearly choke on my food.

"Ma called you?"

"No, I called her."

"…"

"But you are not me. And you know you will always have me. No matter what you decide."

I leap up from my chair, rush to her, and hold her tight.

Memory Castle – Míriam Toyama

(Genre: Drama)

A memory castle, they said. Built in your mind and you'll never lose anything again; it will be all organized and tucked in little corners of your brain. It will all be there, always available. But now the walls of my castle are crumbling down. The doors all look the same. The drawers are empty and the floors are covered in papers and things. I can't seem to find my way out. I can't seem to find myself. I don't remember who I am or who I was.

Mercy – Jon Casper

(Genre: Drama)

I step from the train, unfolding the worn photo ripped from *Time* magazine, where I finally learned her name. The three decades since Desert Storm have been unkind to Fatimah, but her unforgettable eyes still bore into my chest.

The savory aroma of sambuseh permeates the sweltering Iranian afternoon as I thread the streets of Dorud. Gahar Avenue snakes the Sazar River, dropping me in Cheshmeh Sarnajeh as the sun meets the western hills.

These mud-brick buildings haunt my nightmares. Sweep and secure. Gunfire rattling. Doors kicked in on moonless nights. The glowing streak of RPGs under starlit skies. The thrum of artillery.

Out of habit, I scan the rooftops, evoking still darker phantoms.

The Abdali firefight had raged for hours, leaving only two survivors: me and the enemy I'd pinned into a second-floor apartment. Out of ammo, I dashed upstairs with my bayonet, determined to avenge my fallen brothers.

I found the first corpse slumped on the steps — an adolescent — his Tabuk hugged tightly against his body, gunsmoke still drifting from the barrel. I pushed open the door, recoiling from the salty copper stench of blood.

Stepping over the eighth lifeless child, I confronted the reaper who'd annihilated my squad, an AK-47 quaking in her hands.

The girl couldn't have been thirteen, but her eyes had

seen more than mine ever will. Her faded hijab, encircling a face whose trauma belied her youth, had probably once been red as the blood that soaked her thawb. She babbled something I couldn't understand, trigger finger twitching.

I dropped my blade, raised my palms, braced.

Then, inexplicably, she glared at me, lowered her weapon, and retreated into shadow.

Spared.

"Pardon." A young man patiently steers a wheelbarrow around me in the street. "You are needing help?"

Shaken from the past, I muster a smile. "Salam aleikum." Cringing at my appalling Farsi, I retrieve the picture from my pocket. "Is she here?"

His brow furrows as he studies the photo.

"Please." I press my hands together as if in prayer. "I must find her."

He nods toward the homes to my left. "Fatimah."

Beyond a vegetable garden, familiar eyes peek at me from a doorway.

Our jaws fall open together as she and I both utter, "You."

#

Time and distance have starved my apology. Through tears, my words seem emaciated, inadequate. Our encounter surely haunts her as it does me. "We didn't know it was an orphanage. I … I can't shake the nightmares."

Fatimah pours us glasses of chai, and we drop onto low stools beside a potbelly stove. Sunset bathes the room orange, much like the glow from Abdali, set ablaze after my extraction.

"Be not burdened." Her smile buoys my heart. "All is forgiven. Drink."

The chai is earthen and spicy. I swallow greedily.

Then my vision doubles, the room spins, and my stomach knots.

As the light goes out of the world, I glance at my tea and silently thank Fatimah for her second act of mercy.

Matryoshka Doll – Deidra Whitt Lovegren

(Genre: Horror)

Half-awake in the dark, Svetlana adjusted Sergei's silky sheets, now entangled in them hours after their lovemaking. She'd tried to soothe his anger over her drunken flirtations.

The night had grown stale. Her lungs longed for fresh air.

Attempting to sit up, she struck her head on a low, satin-lined ceiling. She felt the narrow enclosure in a frenzied panic.

Kicking — punching — panting, she thrashed the flimsy coffin lid to bits. Extending her arm, her bloodied fingers met the cold ceramic of refractory bricks.

Before hearing a faint "whoosh."

Before smelling sulfur.

Before seeing the spark of ignition.

Midnight at the Ouachita River Bridge – Robert Burns

(Genre: Horror)

Boudreaux hears it long before he sees it—a clanking, rusting echo in the inky woods beyond the halo of streetlight. He scours the dark with bleary eyes until the night insects chitter the car's arrival at the desolate bridge.

The jalopy wheezes to a stop at the tollbooth.

Boudreaux leans in, shudders.

A child's babydoll poses in the passenger seat—glassy eyes watchful.

The ancient driver offers a crumpled dollar. Boudreaux stares transfixed and mechanically passes the vehicle through, taillamps flickering scarlet over the bridge into lonely blackness.

He smooths out the bill and reads the scrawled note.

Help me.

Midnight in Akihabara – thomas iannucci

(Genre: Slice of Life)

You stumble out of the izakaya bar bleary-eyed, which gives everything around you a pleasant haze, diffusing the lights of the city so that they glint and gleam like a kaleidoscope. Around you, passersby studiously avoid eye contact, partly due to the nature of Japanese culture, but also because not wanting to deal with a clearly intoxicated foreigner is a cross-cultural instinct. You laugh at that thought, which you realize probably doesn't help your image, which only makes you laugh harder. A man glances at you and gives you a knowing smile, as if he's been there before. You grin and shoot him a thumbs up, but he is already lost in the sea of pedestrians, and anyway you are easily distracted.

Your attention drifts to another group, friends perhaps, or maybe a blended family, and you wonder what they're doing out this late at night: two men, American most likely, one middle aged, and one in his late twenties. Two women accompany them, both about a decade or so older than the younger man, and they are Japanese. The younger man and the women are all dressed well according to their cultures, though the women are more tastefully understated, one with black hair, the other dyed brown, while the young man is more flashy, his aloha shirt bright red and his tattoos tribal. The older man is dressed for comfort and utility: t-shirt, jeans, a Yomiuri Giants baseball hat. He is clearly leading them somewhere, and his eyes remain focused and vigilant, unlike the rest of them. The women are slower, ever trailing behind the men, so the younger of the two stops and waits for them.

There are two children with the women as well, hence their slowness, both young girls, one a toddler, the other no older than five. The squirmy toddler requires both women to restrain her, with amused grace and no small effort. The older girl clings tightly to the younger man's hand, and he talks warmly with her despite the cold night air and the obvious language barrier. When the toddler gets cranky, he pauses to play with and tease her. She stops crying then, a reaction the other man and the women had not managed to achieve. They amble across the street, unhurried despite the lateness of the hour.

You watch them for a while, captivated by their warmth against the stark, cold night. Then one of the women glances at you, and you smile, but she averts her gaze, pulling the girl closer to her, as if to protect her from the drunken gaijin. You frown and blink and remember why you are drunk at midnight in Akihabara to begin with, and by then they are gone, as lost in the night as you are.

Miner's Retirement – Anne-Marie Kofoed

(Genre: Sci-Fi)

His steel-plated boot kicked up swirls of red dust. Zeez tightened his grip on the heavy sack, the precious load clinking.

"Jeez, Zeez, how much did you find this time?" Milo's scratchy voice interrupted his pace.

"Enough."

"Finally got tired of this place?" Milo took a large swig of his Ruby Beer through the attached straw in his survival suit. Zeez cringed – it cost two ounces of Stella per bottle.

"Can you blame me?"

Milo swept his arm towards the desolate landscape. "But what's not to like?"

Zeez continued towards the DreamZone, its dome rising above them. Stepping into the structure's shadow, relief rushed through him. Decades of hacking through red dust, without a speck of green in sight. An endless hunt for a better world.

"See you on the other side." Milo clapped Zeez's shoulder.

Zeez walked backwards as he replied, "You won't ever bother to find enough for a ticket."

Milo tapped his temple. "You got that right."

"Your loss," Zeez mumbled and approached the reception desk inside.

Zeez lifted the sack onto the scale, and for the first time

in years, a smile broke on his face as the number reached 23.5.

"For a ticket to the DreamZone, you'll need a minimum of 10 pounds in Stella crystals" The receptionist swiped on her screen. "Anything above will give you extras in there."

"Right." Zeez took the ticket and prepared himself for a peaceful life on Mars 2.0, the virtual reality version.

Night Raider – Cindy Strube

(Genre: Suspense)

Silver-edged clouds cloak the full moon, lending just enough light. It's late enough for your plan to work. You advance, moving like a tightrope walker.

Sliding a key into the lock, you cock an ear to the door. Not a sound comes from within.

Click. The tumblers turn. Again, you wait. Holding a small box—and your breath—you ease the door open.

There she is, her shadowy form defenseless in the dark. You do what you must, with synchronized movement.

Slipping your hands beneath her feathers, you remove five warm eggs and tuck five tiny balls of fluff under her wings.

No Sugar this Morning – Del Griffith

(Genre: Drama)

Kafka judges me as I read his words. He tells me that a Texan with a persistent drawl can never understand him. He wouldn't be so severe if I were Czech.

My coffee pot never judges me.

Kafka and Keurig slip into my coffee cup. What they have in common distresses me.

My head buzzes from too much caffeine and too few answers. I think I should stick to reading Spinoza. Contemplating the nature of God and man is much easier on the soul.

My wife comes up behind me and kisses my cheek before she wraps her arms around me. "Can't you just watch porn like all the other guys?"

"Who says I don't?" I put Kafka down, preferring her to his disheartening words.

"Touché, good sir."

She seats herself next to me and sips her coffee. She looks tired, but content. A neat trick that I have yet to master.

"Do you ever think about our life together?" The question escapes my lips before I have a chance to stop it.

My wife smiles at me; perfect teeth emerge over the rim of her cup. "Of course. I tend the garden. You tend the cattle and poach the occasional deer. Our advanced degrees prepared us for this, yes?"

Sarcasm. My wife is the richest natural resource of it.

"And that's it?"

She nods with a certainty that comforts me. "A perfect life, sweetie. The desire for more is madness."

She's right, of course. I blame my mood on her pregnancy and the fear of being my own worst enemy.

I kiss my wife before leaving, stomping a cockroach on the way out.

On Contrition and Shades of Umber – Claire Lindsey

(Genre: Fantasy)

As the north sun rose and the sky filled with birds of fire, I patted my brushes dry and set a clean white canvas on an easel. My wrinkled fingers danced over the labels on my paint collection—shelves filled from floor to ceiling with more colors than most humans would ever see. I lingered at one of the clear glass jars and pulled it from its place. Umber. It reminded me of earth, dried blood and guilt.

I took my time selecting a brush, laying down a thick coat of culpability. Once I'd stained the canvas from top to bottom, I walked away to let it dry. I brewed two cups of tea, regarding my subject carefully as the water bubbled over the fire.

He was young, much younger than my usual clientele, his spirit stretched taut between boy and man. He stared out the window, shoulders hunched inward like an animal curling away from a predator. Perhaps it was his youth, or his quiet demeanor. Something in him made me think of a different soul—one I'd known and loved decades ago.

I offered him some tea, which he eyed but did not touch.

"I am not sure what you have heard about witches," I smiled thinly, "but we rarely meddle in poisons."

He took the cup with a nod, but did not bring it to his lips until mine was empty.

"Tell me why you are here."

My client shifted in the old wooden chair, picking at loose bits of skin along his nail beds, which were already shredded and scabbed. I examined the paint jars, ultimately deciding on a thin shade of ash. Pale and gray like reluctance. I set it beside my brushes and waited. A confession made in haste would help neither of us.

"I set fire to my father's barn," he said.

Expressionless, I searched the shelves for the next color. My fingers wrapped around a jar which was always warm to the touch: pyre. With a wince, I set it down beside the canvas.

"Go on," my voice caught. I glanced at him and had to look away, noting a peculiar familiarity in the way the light cast shadows on his brow.

He talked for a long time, a tale I'd heard in every hue imaginable. A distant father. A long-dead mother. A new and tempestuous woman. I began to paint, adding new colors as I went. I pulled shades of timber and smoke, golden temptation, embers, the sickly coal of hatred. Upon the canvas, a likeness started to form. I filled in cheekbones and thin lips, dark hair and a falsely resolute brow. When I came to the space where his eyes were meant to be, I paused. The eyes were always the hardest, for that was where I painted the sin.

He told me about the lantern, the sweetly familiar scent of hay, consumed by the odor of tallow and smoke. The barn went up easily, he said. He took a sip of tea, long since gone cold. The cup shook in his hand.

"I didn't know," he whispered. His face twisted and contorted, his lips trembled. "If I had known—"

"What happened?"

"The fire spread," he confessed, gasping at the air as if it was filled with smoke. "The house—I couldn't stop it."

My guilt-stained hands found the final color, the one I needed to finish the portrait. Blood. I opened it, dipped a clean brush into the congealed paint.

His voice crumbled. "They were inside."

My brush paused a hair's breadth from the canvas. I met the gaze of the empty, pitch-colored pupil before me and could not tell if I was staring into it, or if it was staring into me. For a moment I imagined flipping the easel, casting the boy out. I had done it before, though only with the most unforgivable of crimes. Before I cast judgment, I stepped back from the portrait and examined it closely, searching the boy's half-dry likeness for putrid shades of malice.

Instead, I found fear.

I exhaled deeply. The north sun had nearly run its course in the sky. The boy stared out the window, wiping at his puffed cheeks. With a few strokes of my brush and a murmured incantation, I filled the portrait's eyes with a raging fire, consuming two dark figures who held each other tightly as they met their end.

"There." I stepped away. "It's finished."

The boy did not meet his own eyes. "What do I do now?"

I gathered my brushes, began rinsing the paint from them, scrubbing it from my fingers. Other colors filled my mind, cerulean and bitter midnight. Swirling shades of grief.

"Destroy it," I said.

"That-that's all?"

I nodded, eyes fixed on the clouded water before me. "Once it is destroyed, you will have your absolution."

The terse line of his shoulders softened. He filled his lungs with clean air. "Thank you."

He took the painting gingerly, careful not to look too long. We did not say farewell.

It took me many hours to clean the remaining brushes and stretch a new canvas. I coated the cloth thickly in white and set it out to dry overnight in preparation for the next day's work. By the time I was done, a contemplative cobalt sky glimmered through the window. I lit a candle and walked the familiar hallways of my home, the wooden floors worn down by decades of my shuffling footfalls. The curtain at the end of the hall knew me as well as I knew it. At my touch, the black velvet material seemed to shiver in anticipation of our nightly ritual.

Breath held tightly, I pulled the cloth back and greeted the painting it concealed. The face which stared back at me was younger, but my own. Raven curls and a sharp, bird-like nose. I raised my candle to the corner of the canvas, watching the paint bubble at the heat. One glance into my eyes, churning with the infinite hues of the sea, and I pulled the candle away. There, where my pupils should be, floated a dark figure whom I once loved more than life.

One Million Silenced Voices – Chris Morris

(Genre: Drama)

That's where they killed Mother.

Dried blood stains the floorboards that concealed us. Where Mother bravely ushered us. Her dead eyes stared through those cracks for days. I was eight; Sonia, three.

We hadn't returned in years. Now, it's best to face it. Honour Mother.

Holding hands, we wander the rooms. The Interahamwe broke more than our spirits. Father's paintings, torn. Mother's rice jars, smashed. Threads of hatred stitched into the place we called home.

A shattered picture frame. In shards, I see my own reflected eyes match Mother's. I can be brave too.

Mother's eyes will watch over Sonia.

Oopsy Daisy – Míriam Toyama

(Genre: Sci-Fi)

I blew up a planet. I didn't mean to. It just happened. It was an old one, the type with pipes and artificial atmosphere. I went there to fix the plumbing system. I started doing that. But it was connected to the water system, which was connected to the air system and so on. Everything depended on everything: a nightmare. You understand? Then there was a spark, or several. The next minute it was in flames. Who knew planets were so flammable? Then it reached the core. It exploded. Oopsy Daisy. I saw it from my ship. It was beautiful.

Phillipa – Anna Sharples

(Genre: Elegy)

Your eyes are

Rimmed with pity,

Veined with understanding.

The potency robs me of a heart beat.

And your face is

Kind. Malleable.

It reflects the pain I feel.

I turn away; I cannot stand the heart ache.

You've watched me

Far too long;

You've really come to know me.

I strain against the soon approaching heart break.

And later—

After—

When your gaze has faded

To a phantom sting,

The emotions still play upon my heart strings.

Prom Night Redux – Robert Burns

(Genre: Drama)

Jacob lay on tousled sheets watching Alana reapply her lipstick.

Candy apple red.

Her periwinkle eyes caught his in the mirror. She giggled.

"What?" he smiled back.

"When was the last time?"

"Remember Prom Night?"

With a final adjustment of her skin-tight dress, Alana returned to the bed. Jacob raised up with puckered lips.

She kissed his cheek. "Bye, baby."

In one fluid motion, Alana snatched her purse from the chair and slung it over her shoulder. She scooped up the cash atop the bureau on her way out.

"Don't be a stranger," Jacob whispered, watching the door close behind her.

Rodney's Bucket – Michał Przywara

(Genre: Drama)

Just what was Rodney hiding in his bucket? It's all we talked about since he burst into class late, swinging the white thing by its handle and whistling.

But every time we asked "What's in the bucket?" he said "Not telling," and then grinned like he was real proud of himself, like he aced a test everyone else bombed. No wonder he didn't have friends. Tyler called him a wanker, but Mrs. Doyle heard him and sent him to the principal. And Rodney? He just grinned harder.

He took the bucket everywhere, and so we followed. Between classes, through the halls, to the playground at recess – where he went, we thundered after him, like we were tied to the thing, like he pulled us along with it.

It was even worse at lunch. We offered him our snacks and he turned them down. He donkey-laughed and greedily clutched that stupid bucket. Carley even offered her beautiful slice of lemon meringue pie – and everyone knew that Carley's mom made the best pies in the world – and Rodney blew a raspberry.

We tried to sneak peeks into the bucket but it had a lid, and by second recess nobody had seen Rodney lift it even once. "What kind of a psycho puts a lid on a bucket?" Tyler asked. We all knew the answer. "What terrible things is he hiding?"

We had to know, and we came up with a plan. By last class, we stopped looking at the bucket. Rodney kept grinning, but we just gave him the coldest of shoulders, and eventually he lost that stupid grin. We waited for him after school. He must have smelled something was up, because he sprinted right out the doors, and pulled us all after him.

Some of us blocked off the road to his house, and others blocked the field, but Rodney was a good runner and he ran right down the alley. We followed him past the mall and the post office, and then we cut him off again, so he veered into the woods.

The thing is, he almost had us. Turned out he was a really good runner and most of us had given up long before the woods, falling to stitches and gasping. But not everyone. Not Tyler, not Carley. Still, Rodney might even have outrun us all, if not for Greenwood Bluff.

Right near the top, right where we lost our breath, Rodney looked over his shoulder. His foot caught a root. He tripped. It wasn't bad – no more than a scrape – but he lost hold of his bucket, and it flew right over the bluff.

We never heard a person make a sound like Rodney made then, like he just saw his dog get hit by a car. He wailed "No!" over and over between sobs. We left him. As his cries drowned out the wind, as his tears soaked his shirt, we left him.

Sentenced – Suma Jayachandar

(Genre: Romance)

Please don't say I complete you. You're not my sentence.

(Genre: Drama)

In the afternoon, soldiers appeared from the north and entered town. They dragged what was left of a body behind one of the trucks and dumped it near the fountain in the plaza. The ground scattered its dust.

The Captain climbed down. He spun slow in the plaza. As he turned, he rested his dark scrutiny on each resident who stood silent, each with a singular ghost on their face.

The trucks idled diesel fumes. Desert met the heavy sky.

Soldiers walked from townface to townface, inspected each person for lines of defiance in their gaze. They placed one woman in a truck and drove off. The air rumbled, then faded.

One young soldier stayed behind, a boy with one arm. He carried no pistol, no rifle. He wore no hat.

From a window, Jackson watched the plaza. When the truckdust went back to its streetbed, he stepped out. The young soldier's face stood vacant.

Why are you here? asked Jackson.

We won the war, said the young soldier, a boy with one arm, cut off from companions and amputated from completeness.

No. Why are *you* here? Alone?

The boy inhaled deeply, paused, pushed out a hot lungful of desert air. *Melcher*, he said.

What do you know of him? asked Jackson. Thomas

Melcher was a fighter who had disappeared several days earlier. Word had spread through the towns.

He was my father.

Jackson stood silent for a moment, then pointed to the mess the soldiers had dumped by the fountain.

Is that him? he asked.

Young Melcher nodded and looked around at the townfaces that, bearded and sunbrown and furrowed, stared back.

I'm worthless now, he said.

First a traitor and now a sacrifice, said Jackson.

The townfaces tightened their circle, one step, two. Their boots raised small clouds of dust.

Jackson raised his palm to the crowd. They stopped.

How did you lose your arm? he asked.

Young Melcher clenched his teeth, put his fist to his mouth.

Not lost, he said. Taken.

The sun sighed a burning breeze. A large bird descended to the body by the fountain. Another.

Are you going to fight? asked Jackson.

The boy Melcher lowered his fist, but kept it tight. Would there be a point? he said.

No, said Jackson. We are many.

The townface tightened its circle again.

Melcher looked around. Will it help? he asked.

What?

When you kill me, will it help you forget?

No, said Jackson. Dust still blows over our graves.

True. All carried headstones in their hearts. Kindness had bled itself dry into the earth.

It could have helped, said a townface that came closer, separated itself from the crowd, and became the face of a young woman with a scar on her cheek. It could have helped, she said, if we hadn't lost so much.

The townfaces muttered as one and tapered into silence. For a few seconds, nobody moved. Then, by the fountain, the birds ripped the stillness open.

Young Melcher exhaled his few years.

Yours too was taken, he said.

Jackson nodded. Something they had in common with the boy.

Yet it wasn't enough. Whether theft was loss or whether loss swept into a town in dusty trucks didn't much matter to Jackson nor to the townfaces. What mattered stood as delegate before them with one arm that dangled and another that rested somewhere in a wheelbarrow of limbs.

It may not have been as they deeply wished, not as they had once revered, but at times expediency and ease rose from mere shadows of dusty rain. And, as they had all observed, each on their own private calendar of sorrow, at times justice simply stood outside the tightening circle of condemnation, and let justification have its very own festal day.

Silence – Thom Brodkin

(Genre: Romance)

There is a peace at sunrise that surpasses all understanding. It's a renewal. A feeling that anything is possible. I'd like to say I drag myself from the comfort of my bed every day to enjoy the sunrise's splendor, but you wouldn't believe me and I would be lying. What is true is I was there that day and so was she.

There is a connection between sunrisers just because they are sunrisers. It's a shared, yet unspoken, appreciation for things quiet and beautiful. That might explain why I was immediately drawn to her, but I know it wasn't just because of the earliness of the morning. Delilah, you see, would have attracted me no matter the time of day. The first time I saw her I was sitting there, at my favorite secret spot, overlooking Lake Quinault.

It's a hidden gem in Washington State owned by the Quinault Indian Nation and, before that day, if I had had my way, no one would ever have sat and admired its beauty other than me.

The lake, a destination point for fishermen, swimmers, and sightseers, is nature at its most spectacular. It is located deep in the Olympic National Forest. It isn't easy to find, even if you're looking for it. Once discovered, even the most magnanimous outdoorsmen will keep the secret to themselves. In an era where, too often, free time is wasted in front of a flat screen TV, Lake Quinault is a reminder of the reasons for taking vacations and the sunrise over the lake is God's definition of must-see.

That particular trip occurred in early summer. I remember it vividly because I had to be in place just after 5:00 a.m. to catch the sun as it appeared over the mountain. Summer is the best time to watch the sunrise because no one in their right mind would be up early enough, nor would be hardy enough to make the journey to my secret spot. No one except me, and Delilah.

Is this seat taken?

Not many people can remember the first words spoken by or to the love of their life, but I absolutely can. That morning, as I turned to see from where the unexpected voice was coming, the first light of dawn revealed the most beautiful girl I had ever seen. Not all men might have thought so. Delilah wore no makeup, a pair of ripped jeans, and a faded brown hoodie. Her hair, perfectly auburn, looked as if it hadn't been touched since she'd rolled out of bed that morning. It was obvious she had made no effort to look beautiful and yet she had an inner spark that couldn't be hidden. Not by tattered jeans or a faded hoodie. Something changed that first moment I saw her; I changed. I had spent years guarding my secret spot, and now, surprisingly, unexpectedly, delightfully, I wanted nothing more than to share my sunrise with her.

I, unfortunately, was not born a poet and as such the most romantic thing I could think of in response to her inquiry was: It's a free country. With that, she invaded my secret spot, both next to the lake and in my heart.

The silence that followed was both loud and revealing. Delilah wasn't there for small talk; she was there to admire the beauty of sunrise. We sat in silence and watched as the sun peeked over the horizon, covering the two of us in its warming light. She and I carried on a conversation without words. She told me, silently, that she understood the importance of the moment, and I responded in kind that this moment was made all the more special because she was there to share it.

Perfection is a goal impossible to realize in this mortal realm, but that morning came as close as is humanly possible. So many thoughts ran through my mind as the sun revealed itself completely. Then just as quickly and quietly as she had come, Delilah rose to her feet, wiped some residual dirt from the seat of her ripped jeans, and headed down the trail and out of my sight.

Eight words verbalized, an infinite number of potential events contemplated. Thirty minutes had passed, a lifetime had been imagined. I was sure I would never see her again, and the thought made me overwhelmingly sad.

The next five years came and went, five long years since that day at the lake. There were first dates, first kisses, and the words I love you exchanged, yet every time fate or intention would reach down and sabotage promise. I became determined to find peace in my solitude.

There was always a reason or an excuse for my ending every potential relationship, but at its core was a shared sunrise and a conversation that didn't happen.

I went to our spot from time to time, to see the sunrise, not for her. At least, that's what I told myself. I had given up without realizing I was hoping. Hoping to see her again. Hoping to feel what I felt that day. Hoping she would be there. And then it happened. It was once again summer, it was sunrise, but this time she was there.

Is this seat taken?

It's a free country.

The same eight words.

At the time, I didn't know that she, too, had often made the trip back to our secret spot.

Seeing her again, I knew I wouldn't let the opportunity slip from my grasp, not a second time.

When the sun had completed its part in our play, Delilah rose to her feet and wiped the dirt from her jeans exactly as she had done five years earlier. This time, however, I stood up as well.

My name is Peter. I don't like coffee, but I'd really like to have a cup with you.

My name is Delilah, she responded, matter-of-factly, and I would be glad to share a cup of Joe.

She called it Joe? It's funny the things that confirm that a love is real. I couldn't tell her that day, for fear of losing her, but at that moment, I was sure. I had said I love you to others before, but it was obvious to me that I had lied. For in that moment, I was finally sure what love felt like.

Lifetimes are only lifetimes when viewed in reverse. A cup of coffee became a dinner date. A dinner date became a commitment. A commitment became a proposal, and a proposal became forever. There were kids and dogs and vacations, but more than anything, there were trips to Lake Quinault. Always at sunrise. Always just the two of us. Never any words spoken.

You never know the last time is the last time until it's too late. The final trip we took to Lake Quinault was like all the rest. It took a little longer for tired, old bones to make the trek, but we found our spot, sat together, and conversed in silence. The sun, unaffected by time, rose as perfectly as always, but Delilah rose only with my help.

Would you like to share a cup of Joe?

She knew I did. She knew sitting next to her pretending to like coffee was my greatest pleasure.

She also knew she would never come back to see another sunrise even though I was too stubborn to admit it to myself.

That day in the café we told stories of family and friends, living and lost, as we sipped on what had eventually become my favorite beverage. We made a mental scorecard of our life and realized we had won.

Two days later I lost her. Just like that first day at the lake, I watched her as she left me alone, this time without even the hope of returning. The sadness I felt from years back flooded over me like a tidal wave.

I'll save a seat for you. Those were her last words to me. True to myself, I replied: It's a free country. Then, she was gone.

One day, hopefully soon, I will watch the sunrise with my Delilah again only from a far better secret place. Until then, I only go to our special spot at night.

I'm never alone when I go there. I make my way to our clearing and sit down just as I did all those years ago. As the moon reflects off the lake, I feel her comforting hand reach down for me, and in the silence only we understand, I hear her very clearly.

Spoon Theory – Cindy Strube

(Genre: Suspense)

I have been poisoned.

That, Dear Reader, was my last coherent thought before passing out in the five-star restroom of *Bistrot Le Coquillage.*

(I pause here to remark that no one at that worthy establishment is to blame for the events that… well, read on!)

We haven't had a good French place in town since *L'escargot Beurré* burned down. Those blissful, buttery bites were *sooo* good—but, honestly, how many ways are there to cook a snail? So I was aflutter with anticipation when Pierre (not his real name), our usual waiter from *L'escargot*, whispered word of the coming *bistrot*.

We ran into him at the farmers' market, as we studied a display of artisanal cheeses. He bounced up to us, aquiver with Gallic emotion.

"M'sieur! Madame!" he exclaimed, "'ave you 'eard? There is to be a new *bistrot*! I 'ave accepted the position of 'ead waiter! I will be expecting your visit, *oui?*"

You've probably experienced, if you're anything of a gourmand, that restaurant workers circulate among the various establishments like frozen berries in a blender.

For example: Antonio, your favorite chef at *Nostra Cucina,* disappears. His replacement, Flavio, is an excellent chef—but he doesn't have the touch when it comes to seasoning the calamari batter just right. So you try out *Mangiare Bene* as soon as it opens, hoping against hope. You, almost resigned to sub-par seafood, order the "house" *calamari fritti*. Your expectations low, you await them with glum spirit.

The five golden rings arrive, exquisite in texture and taste. In the subtle, sea-flavored, lemon-scented masterpiece, you recognize the art of... Antonio.

Such is the close-knit community of food lovers. We all know each other, don't we?

Excuse the sidetrack. Back to the anticipatory fluttering.

Early on, I was advised on some crucial rules of restaurant reviewing.

One: Go incognito. You don't want the staff to make a special effort to impress, knowing you're a food writer.

Two: Always attend with a small group.

Three: Never visit a new establishment on opening night.

Rule three: Gave *Bistrot Le Coquillage* a full two weeks to set their pace.

Rule two: Recruited my husband and an eclectic group of foodie friends.

Rule one: Requested one of them to reserve a table in his name.

And off we went—eight eager epicures expecting extraordinary edibles.

(Pardon—couldn't resist!)

The *bistrot* occupies the old bus depot downtown. Don't let that put you off; it has been transformed. Not a whiff of motor oil to be smelt.

The exterior has been freshly painted in a warm, peachy

shade, and draped with miniature twinkly lights. Very inviting!

We stepped through the rustic oaken door into a bustling, intimate interior packed with patrons. The air was infused with an exquisite symphony of aromas.

There was a buzz of conversation, the clink of cutlery, and the familiar voice of Pierre.

"Ah!" He clasped his hands together, beaming a smile so bright we could almost feel the warmth. "Welcome! You will not, I promise you, be disappointed!"

I won't linger on my description of the interior. Clean, cozy, tasteful. Celadon green table linens overlaid with cheery toppers in a pretty Provençal pattern. Quality art prints featuring the French countryside. More twinkly lights strung along the ceiling alcove. Altogether charming.

But our focus is the food!

What could be a better start than a fresh-baked baguette, still warm from the oven? Denny, the busboy (who used to work at *Chloe's Creamery and Sandwich Shop* before its unfortunate demise) brought a board and knife. Pierre followed, carrying a swaddled bundle of pure gustatory joy, which he sliced up right under our noses. (Oh dear—I'm not sure that's the right image. But I'll leave it in.)

Side note: Fresh baguettes *must* be served with imported European butter. And *Bistrot Le Coquillage* does just that.

Now, down to business. Dear Reader, put on your deerstalker and get out your notebook. Let's see if you can follow the clues in the bill of fare and solve a mystery.

The menu is not overburdened with selections, but there's

something suitable for every guest. We chose a variety of dishes to share:

To begin, a salad of field greens featuring crumbly aged *chèvre,* dried currants, and nasturtium petals. It was lightly dressed, with a citrusy finish. I suspected the presence of bergamot, which could be a risky ingredient—in the sense that it's a polarizing flavor. I happen to love it.

Next, wild chanterelle soup in a clear garlicky broth, garnished with thyme leaves and shaved fennel. Denny stepped up once more, offering a twist or three of cracked pepper so fresh it made my olfactory glands tingle!

We chose two sides: a simple dish of sauteed leeks, and a more complex one of roasted root vegetables whipped up with crème fraîche.

If you've never tried chicken *Chasseur* (Hunter's chicken), here's your opportunity. Tender *poulet*, stewed with tomatoes and tarragon, it is French comfort food. As is ham and bean cassoulet. The *bistrot* enhances their version of cassoulet with pork skin and duck fat. Flavorful and filling!

But the pinnacle of this meal was a gratin of sea scallops. Pan seared in clarified butter, they were presented in bubbling, cheesy cream sauce scattered with fried sage leaves and breadcrumbs. The aroma was indescribable, and a little unsettling.

Wanting to savor the decadence, I cut a tender morsel in two and popped a portion into my mouth. Saliva welled up in my throat as I chewed. The scallops were cooked to perfection; the sauce was superb—and this was the wrong kind of salivating.

The murmur of voices receded, and my brain felt foggy.

I grabbed my water goblet with a shaking hand and took a quick gulp.

I squirmed in my chair. I was really beginning to feel unwell.

Pushing my plate away, I stood up. The other scallop sat untouched.

"Excuse me…"

I headed to the back, squeezing past the tightly packed tables. My hearing was muffled, and my vision blurry. I wasn't sure I'd make it to the restroom in time.

Surely the feeling had come on too soon to be caused by contaminated food… No one else seemed to feel sick… Was I coming down with a virus?

I pushed the door open, stumbled into the ladies' room, and proceeded to be violently ill.

I was alone in the room, retching and vomiting until I felt the room begin to spin.

Professional food critics are a dying breed, but I don't want to die this way!

And as the dark curtain descended, I knew—

I have been poisoned.

~~~

What a commotion I caused!

Dear Reader, I opened my eyes to find strangers hovering over me. They wore navy blue… uniforms? Two men and a woman. Paramedics? … Where was I?

It turned out that I was still in the ladies' room of *Bistrot*
~~~

Le Coquillage, stretched out on the celadon settee.

From there, the team took me to the hospital. I was hydrated, questioned, examined, and tested. My husband and our friends were grilled.

"Well," said Dr. Lozano at last, "we think we know the cause."

Dear Reader, can you guess?

Was it listeria in the greens? The wrong kind of mushroom in the soup? But—remember, the attack came on rather suddenly, and no one else got sick…

"You have developed tropomysin sensitivity."

I was shocked! I can no longer eat shellfish, or at least bivalve mollusks, which contain an allergenic type of the protein. There is no treatment, just avoidance.

What a tragedy for a food writer!

It could be worse though. Apparently, my body has just decided that particular protein is an enemy, to be rejected immediately. I don't experience anaphylaxis, just very unladylike emesis.

But enough of that.

~~~

I believe in second chances. So, after some weeks, we made arrangements to revisit *Bistrot Le Coquillage*. (Though its very namesake has become my nemesis, the fine establishment has plenty of other delightsome dishes.)

This time, I broke all available rules.

"This is Sadie Darnell. I'd like to make reservations for two… Yes, I'm *that* Sadie Darnell."
~~~

Pierre greeted us with open arms. He actually hugged me.

"Ah, *Madame*! 'ow good to see you again, looking well!"

He presented the menu, and then asked, "Would you like to 'ear tonight's specials?"

We nodded.

"We 'ave two choices. There is grilled lamb chop with garlic confit and sauce *persillade*. And there is…" Pierre stopped. His face drained of color, and he looked at me with mournful eyes. "Ah… I cannot recommend to you the second special, *Madame*!"

We both chose the lamb. If you are fortunate enough to visit on a night when lamb is offered, you must try it! The bright, almost sharp parsley flavor is a perfect counterpoint to the richness of lamb and roasted garlic.

Oh, and—when you do go, be sure to save room for a few *petit* pastries to end your meal.

They're to die for! ★ ★ ★ ★ ★

© 2024 Sadie Darnell for *The Daily Dish*

So Doth the Widow Weep – Chris Morris

(Genre: Romance)

I wander the rocky shore, my ship in pieces behind me

The storm had shaken its core, my crewmates are lost to the sea.

A flash of lightning above me, I search for a warm place to dry

Through the rain there seems to be a lighthouse that beams to the sky.

And through the fearsome gale, a beautiful sound I hear

It makes me feel less frail, and washes away most of my fear.

> *'Singing o, where is my true love?*
>
> *'He was lost to the clamorous sea*
>
> *'O, where be my true love?*
>
> *'One day he'll come back for me.'*

The haunting voice drifts down from the highest part of the lighthouse

In its tone I blissfully drown, its rapturous fires I can't douse.

I'm happily entranced by the sound, I feel I must meet its owner

For her beauty must be renowned, and up there she must feel like a loner.

I climb the rocky face that separates me from the melody

As my heart begins to race, her voice is my misery's remedy.

> *'Singing o, be that my true love?*
>
> *'Coming back at long last to me?*
>
> *'O, are you my true love?*
>
> *'Escaped from the treacherous sea?'*

Inside the lighthouse is dim; I ascend each crumbling stair

The lantern room is grim; it's cold and remarkably bare.

Above me the light shines bright; I'm in awe of its ominous glow

I worry that something's not right; and wonder if perhaps I should go.

At the window she stands with a frown, staring out at the iniquitous sea

She wears an elegant gown, and she turns and sings to me.

> *'Singing o, here is my true love!*
>
> *'You've left the perilous sea*
>
> *'O, thank you my true love!*
>
> *'You've finally come for me.'*

I take her hand in mine; it's as cold as the roaring sea

I tell her: 'All will be fine, but you've sadly mistaken me.

'For I am not who you say, the man you search for with sorrow

'And though I'd love to stay, I think you may fade on the morrow.'

Her eyes fall to the floor, a cold tear descending her cheek

She begins her song once more; this time her voice is meek.

At once it comes to me; I've known her most of my life

I once got down on one knee and asked her to be my wife.

Serendipitous be death for us both; the lighthouse brings us together

I swear an undying oath; I'll be with my dearest forever.

How fortunate here be this light that summons lost souls to its call

For now as all turns to white, I feel no sense of sadness at all.

Singing o, she is my true love

She rescued me from the sea

O, here be my true love

She set my glad heart free.

The After War – Trevor Woods

(Genre: Drama)

"Hey, Ben?"

Everyone in the budget meeting gawks as Ben's boss attempts to elicit a response. Still unaware, Ben continues staring blankly through the high-rise window. The corporate conference room bland enough not to offend anyone's cultural sensibilities is a stark contrast from the Arabian desert.

Ben's thinking about his best friend Sergeant First Class (SFC) Liam Foster's family.

His therapist warned in his last session that over-prioritizing others' well-being more than his own could eventually kill him. Easier said than done—Foster's death in Iraq two years ago still feels like it happened yesterday.

"Ben!" His boss raises his tone.

Ben quickly turns, now offering his attention. "Huh?"

"Where did you go, bud?" His boss teases while thumbing the pages of the monthly finance report.

His co-workers giggle.

"Oh, I thought it was beer-thirty." Ben's reply transforms everyone's giggles into laughs. His coworkers adore his knack for injecting levity and humor into any situation. They also love his selflessness, which was ingrained in him over a 20-year military career—being a team player, almost always to a fault.

After the meeting, Ben's boss stops him in the hall. "Hey,

are you good? You seem off this week."

"I just got some stuff going on at home—nothing to worry about." Ben smiles, hoping for no further questions. *In the business world, the personal and professional must be separated*, he reminds himself. Ben has become well-practiced at wearing his mask at work.

"Okay, let me know if you need time off… It's not a problem." His boss offers a friendly pat on the shoulder, then escapes the conversation.

Back in the Army, this situation would have played out differently. When any of his Army buddies were a little *off*, it would constitute a "bar run." They'd drag them out to the local bars for drinks, spiritedly harass them, and give bad dating advice. Sometimes that bad advice was exactly what they needed.

However, the advice wasn't the point, it was the brotherhood who gave it. The mantra, *leave no soldier behind*, wasn't just for soldiers at war, it was a mantra for life.

The most-equipped people that can help cure the wounds of war are a soldier's brothers-in-arms. Folks outside of that circle have their own priorities and families to tend to.

After an eight-hour workday as a salaried project manager, his drive home is a waking dream he barely recollects. Somehow, his deep reflections are compartmentalized while his brain's motor functions autopilot him home safely. His loss of purpose and camaraderie, which Army provided, unmoored him. Preparing the monthly finance report fails to fulfill him like saving innocent families from ISIS terrorists in Iraq did.

His attempt to reintegrate back into society was rewarded

by an empty house and child support payments. Luckily, his ex-wife left him the dog.

Ben kneels to greet his Golden Retriever, Sam. "Hey, boy!" Ben's cheeks reach his ears, releasing the tension he accumulated that day as Sam jumps into his arms. Their traditional wrestling session in the foyer always prefaces a doggy-treat and long walk outside. Sam is Ben's only dopamine regulator these days, with most of his old Platoon now retired, lost, or dead. Sam is Ben's lifeline now.

Most nights consist of white styrofoam takeout containers and shots of Maker's Mark, the same whisky his old Platoon drank on the weekends before a sniper took off Foster's head. Lately, Ben's nine-millimeter has been within arms-reach, dark thoughts crossing his mind more times than he would care to admit. He toils above the threshold of the great void regularly. It would be so easy—alcohol and guns never mix well. But Foster's death anniversary isn't like most days because he has an important call to make.

Ben dials the same number he's dialed for the past two years.

She answers, "Hey, Ben!"

"Hey, Jess, how have you been?"

"As good as I can be, I guess. We just got back from Liam's gravesite about an hour ago. You should come next year."

"I… I don't know… Maybe next year. How is Lexi? Did she ask where Foster was for her birthday this year?"

"She did. She still doesn't understand what happened to her dad. It's been over two years, and frankly I'm starting to get worried. This year she had a Blue's Clues birthday, a bouncy house, and her classmates over."

"Sounds awesome. I couldn't make it… work and all."

She waits for Ben to share more details, but he doesn't. He never does.

"Are you okay? We're worried about you."

Ben's lips scrunch as he gazes through the ceiling, his eyes watering. It's becoming harder for him to suppress his suffering. He replies with a faltered voice, a tear streaming down his face. "Yeah, I'm fine. Nothing me and ole' Sam can't handle."

"Well, we're all thinking of you. Thanks for calling. You know, you don't have to wait for his anniversary to call—call anytime."

"I know."

"Okay, have a wonderful night, and pet Sam for us."

"I will."

Ben hangs up the phone, placing it next to his nine-millimeter. He quickly uses his shirt to wipe the sorrow from his face. He looks down at Sam, finding him staring with his puppy-dog eyes, tail wagging, waiting for their walk.

He sits there staring through Sam, still hanging on by a thread. Fortunately, Sam's unrelenting joy pulls him back.

Ben's hollowed face energizes, letting out a heavy sigh. "Okay, boy. Let's go for a walk. How's that sound?" Sam agrees by sprinting to the door, his paws clacking across the hardwood. He sits patiently, albeit with a pathetic whine.

Ben laughs, as the constant, heavy feeling of deadness in his chest dissipates, at least temporarily, at the sight of Sam's enthusiasm.

"You're so easily pleased, boy."

As he grabs Sam's leash, he thinks, *No one told me there would be another war to fight after war.*

He decides he's not done fighting, as Sam leads them both out the door.

Why We Stay Out of Dark Woods – Misty Mator

(Genre: Fairy Tale)

The little witch Yaga did not know where she would go come autumn. She was only boarding with the venerable Mother Holle for the summer (no one would dream of asking to live there in the winter).

"Now, Yaga, it's time."

Young Yaga went out to the barn, for here in the world under the stone well, the chickens were as large as pigs.

Yaga carried the white egg, big as a prince's head, into the kitchen. She put into the pot milk, then a birch log, a pine shingle, and a bone chewed by an obedient dog. When she thought Mother Holle's back was turned, she cut her finger with a winter bone knife and added three drops of her own blood (or was it one? No matter).

When it was boiling, Holle helped Yaga gently lower the egg on a slotted ladle into the brew. Yaga held the egg under the roiling red-brown potion, humming a nursery rhyme. Once the liquid was moon white again, the egg glowed sunset red.

Mother Holle carefully placed the towel-bundled egg into a basket with a door knocker and looked little Yaga straight in the eye.

"Take this, and go back up to your woods in the world above." Mother Holle grinned. "When this hatches, you'll never be homeless again."

In the deep woods, Yaga opened the linen under the dark moon. A small hut with chicken legs splintered out of the shell.

"Come, let's get you some more blood," little Yaga said.

250

The Celestial Matchmakers – Chris Morris

(Genre: Fantasy)

The stars were particularly twinkly tonight. *Twinkly*. A great word. Almost onomatopoeic. The convivial younger cousin of sparkly. One could picture these twinkly stars hanging in a sky that was sure to be serene and beautiful. It popped. It was fun.

Unlike Bruce. That oaf didn't appreciate fun. He had barely smiled one day in his eight-million-year life. The only hint of joy Teenah ever caught in his eye was when he thought he'd beaten her at her own game. Tonight, he obviously thought he'd done it again.

'Look! Look at what I've done, Teenie, you'll never beat that!'

Teenie. The irritating step-sister of *Teenah.* She'd have corrected the doofus if it didn't mean giving him the response he clearly wanted. She peered down at the blue marble below. The scene of every one of these silly battles. Among the clamorous hustle and bustle of vibrant cities and the crashing of great, majestic waves against rocky shores and the fluttering of feathered wings and the rushing of roaring winds, she saw it.

'Is that…?'

'Yup!' Bruce's triumphant, smug little grin settled on his face like a wet piece of clay setting before its artist could correct a slight imperfection. 'A police officer and a criminal.'

Teenah strained her eyes. She peered at the building,

used all her energy to see through its walls and into the cells within. A man in uniform leaned his face through the bars of a cell and kissed the mouth of a blonde-haired lady on the other side.

Teenah gasped. 'But… that's *wrong!* Don't humans have a rule against that sort of thing? That officer will lose his job! Or worse! You have to undo this one!'

Bruce chuckled. 'Ah, come on, Teenie! Sure, it's possible the guy'll lose his job. Might even end up in a cell himself. But that's not important. What's more important than love?'

'You should use your spells more responsibly, Bruce!'

The nincompoop shook his head. 'We won't have to wait long to find out. I predict another page in my book in about sixty human years' time.'

Teenah huffed. She folded her arms across her chest. The pair waited, watched the blue marble spin a thousand days in the blink of one celestial eye. In a single breath, the world before them changed. The oceans became deeper, the humans got livelier, songs were sung and stories were spun and, finally, the officer's and the criminal's time on their planet came to a quiet end. The white guestbook in Bruce's hands became bigger.

Bruce opened to the most recent page. He cleared his throat. 'It says… *Of all the wondrous things we learned of our universe since our hearts stopped beating, the mysterious matchmaker in the sky who brought us together with some extraterrestrial spell might be the most incredible. We don't know why you chose us, Mister Matchmaker, but we thank you, from the heavens to the earth…* Aw, isn't that sweet!'

A fire lit in Teenah's stomach. Without a word, she

narrowed her eyes and found exactly what she was looking for among the infinite chaos of the blue marble. She chanted her incantation and watched. She could feel Bruce at her side gaping at the same part of the planet.

He burst out laughing. 'Too ambitious, Teenie! It'll never work!'

Two opposing soldiers in a grey and fiery battlefield. They'd gotten themselves stuck inside the same ramshackle building, and it was coming down. One of the men stood beneath an entire burning floor that was crumbling. The other man rushed at him, tackled him to the ground, shoved him out of harm's way.

They embraced.

Bruce looked as though a black hole was about to swallow him up. 'It'll never last, though! Never!'

Teenah forced her most confident grin. 'Let's just see, shall we?' In three blinks of an eye, her own guestbook grew an extra page. She flipped it open. *Who'd have thought that love could bloom on a battlefield? That two soldiers from warring nations would one day wed? That some kind of goddess was watching out for us from the sky? Thank you, kind spirit; may your days be as endlessly divine as our love for each other.'*

Bruce's nostrils flared. 'Right, that's it!'

He beamed a flurry of red and green into the marble with all of his force. An environmentalist and an industrial CEO fell in love.

Teenah beamed a spell even harder. Furious yellow sparks flared from her fingertips. A world leader and a clown got married.

All at once, spells were flying downwards at an incredible rate, and Teenah watched with Bruce as more pairs fell for one another. A drug dealer and a nun. A butcher and a vegan. A librarian and a rock star. A cat and a dog.

'*That one's too far, Bruce!*'

Then, as suddenly as it had all started, it came to a stop. Teenah panted. Bruce was doubled over.

Teenah tried to catch her breath. 'It's exhausting, isn't it?'

Bruce nodded. 'Fancy a temporary truce? A tiny break, Teenie?'

The pair lay side by side and gazed into the vast galaxies and ethereal, endless nebulas before them. Sometimes it shook Teenah to the inner workings of her soul. This mesmerising, infinite realm and Teenah's little place within it. In a strange sort of way, it was nice to have someone here to share in the overwhelming awe of it all. Even if it was an imbecile like Bruce.

Still, he wasn't all that bad, was he? Were they really so different? Two celestial rivals, inspiring the best from one another.

She took his hand in hers to make sure he wouldn't disappear into the expanse. That wouldn't do. Not at all. A little rest was all they needed. Two hundred human years or so. That would do the trick.

Sometime in the hundred and seventeenth year, Bruce commented on how twinkly the stars were, and Teenah's grip on his hand tightened. Just a teenie bit.

The Forever-Now of Forest Time – Misty Mator

(Genre: Romance)

"The clearest way into the Universe is through a forest wilderness." – John Muir

I met him in misty Muir Wood.

I shifted my weight on my portable step stool that day, trying to get a better photo of the growth on the side of the redwood tree.

A deep, gentle voice. "That's a burl. Redwoods are unique. They don't just grow from seeds, they grow from those too. If there's a fire or stressor, they create copies of themselves that will grow from those burls. Everything the original tree learned is in the copy's fibers. Like a rebirth."

I looked down from the cloud-high redwoods towards the man. Even on my step stool, he towered over me. He had dark curly hair like wet wood, glowing copper skin, and salient green eyes. He could've been thirty or fifty, and dazzlingly striking. He nodded at my backpack.

"You a photographer?"

"Yeah. I got my daughter safely tucked away at college, and now I'm pursuing *my* old college dream. I'm entering a contest where the grand prize is a travel contract with National Geographic. I thought a photo of tomorrow's eclipse in this timeless forest would make for a unique photo. Sorry." I tried to chuckle. "I'm not sure why I'm telling you all this."

He smiled in a way that used his eyes more than his mouth, lips closed. "That is the way of things. We reach towards each other. Even these great redwoods reach towards each other under the ground. You came here alone, so you reached towards me."

His grin broke open. "I know the perfect place for you to get that photo. I am able to walk off the boarded trails — I can lead you there. Just no photos of me." He looked me over, from my bright-red dyed hair to my boots and up again. I felt a delicious warmth flood through me.

"Your hair looks like fire. If I lead you through the woods, will you burn me?" he jested.

I quirked my eyebrow devilishly at him. "Only if you say *please*."

~~~~~~~

His name was Elswyth. I was way too middle-aged for love at first sight. I kept babbling like an idiot, maybe to compensate for how slowly I followed behind him.

"I wanted my daughter to grow up in one place. I wanted her to feel rooted, you know? Her father wasn't in the picture, and I couldn't be gone all the time, photographing the world. I put my dream on hold for her. Now it's *my* turn for a new start. I think it's that way for a lot of moms."

"It's a good way. You made time-honored choices — both then and now." He treaded widely. "Watch your step."

His words sank into me, flowering a sense of self-worth I'd forgotten I had. I picked my way carefully over the old-growth roots. The scent in the woods was incredible: clean, earthy. Like the smell at the beginning of everything.

"I feel a little like I stepped back in time," I noted aloud, as we worked our way through the mist.
~~~~~~~

"Maybe you have. Redwoods are the past, the present, and the future. They live in a forever-now."

At that, I paused. "Forever-now...I've heard fairyland described like that. And heaven — that, to us, we're waiting to rejoin our loved ones, but in heaven there is no time, all of your loved ones are already there. It's always *now*."

He responded, "Love is deeper than time. In Love, you don't have to be more, be better. Just grow. Be. Reach and love."

"Just what kind of shaman wood-sprite are you anyway?" I laughed, my heart aglow. He looked at me with dancing fire in his minty green eyes — then I fell.

Yes, in love, but literally — I fell. I slipped and began descending, careening downwards, my blood icicled as I looked up at him on the high hillside. He was up there ...then he appeared behind me, arms wrapped around me with leaves budding out of his skin.

I gaped into his green eyes, "How...are you *here*?"

I meant behind me, because the leaves hadn't registered yet, but he answered the bigger question: "The veil is thin at certain times, like when there's an eclipse. I won't be able to walk this world for long after. Not for a while."

I should've felt disbelief, but in that forest? Everything felt possible. I decided that if I was hallucinating or in a fairy tale, I might as well go all the way. I reached for him, and loved, in every way.

~~~~~~~

Time really did seem to move differently. Three days, three weeks, or three years seemed to pass in what must
~~~~~~~

have been just one day. I was happy, and I made him happy. It was enough. I would worry about *later* when it came.

~~~~~~~

Then *later* arrived.

The day of the eclipse, we awoke to cloud cover. We climbed doggedly upward, mud squelching beneath our feet. He could not stay in my world, but I could join him in his. I didn't care about travel photography anymore – who would when you'd found heaven on earth? But I cared about my daughter. I knew from experience, no matter your age, you still need your mom.

My heart dragged, weighed by indecision. He insisted I still try to get the photo. He led me on and said, "Maybe the sky will clear."

Thunder began to shake the ground, the trees groaning. It wasn't the darkness of the eclipse I'd come to photograph, but we were enveloped just the same. He turned towards me with a desperate, fierce longing in his face.

It happened so fast.

A blinding jagged streak in the sky flew at me, and Elswyth seemed to grow impossibly tall and wooden, faster than I could think. I heard a crackling then blacked out.

~~~~~~~

When I awoke, I was sprawled amongst emerald ferns. A redwood stood directly in front of me, with a burned hollow from lightning. Beside it was a new tree...a copy of the original.

(Genre: Drama)

When faced with a fork, look for the twig.

We had missed the twig and were staring down a deep chasm. It didn't help that we were not talking to each other. After the boisterous cultural evening put up by fellow campers, we had fought over which bottle to drink water from, back in our tent. Our sabre-rattling was loud enough for other campers to give me extra sweet smiles at breakfast.

Trekking was not something we had done before in our twenty years of marriage. It was supposed to be an exercise in bonding after our only child had left for college. But as always, the most unexpected things flared up, and as usual, we ended up alone in each other's company.

After breakfast, sixty of us were dropped off at the foot of the hill. The trek captain briefed us and handed us over to a local tribal boy who knew every creek on the hill. Only two parts of that talk remained in my head—Do not disturb the wildlife and meet you all at the top of the hill. He might have also said—When faced with a fork on the trail, choose the path on which a twig is placed by the pilot batch.

We started as a single file but the trekkers who were young or seasoned, or just had hearts lighter than us, sped past us. The hardy shrubs brushed against our bodies at times as we slipped on the path covered by the scattered leaves dampened by the dew. I might have seen a twig or two on the other side of the fork that led us here but chose not to warn my silent partner. I wanted to watch his face burn with shame when he realised his oversight. I thought it would be a sweet revenge.

But now, I am not so sure.

We spy on each other. He is sweating despite the cool morning breeze. I tap the stick in my hand on the gravel and take in the expanse beyond the chasm. The green mounds of western ghats sparkle there, unaffected by two miserable people gazing at them. The sky is overcast, contrary to the weather forecast. We take out bottles from our heavy rookie backpacks and sip water. I choose to break the silence.

"Oops! I think we took a wrong turn."

He glowers.

I take out an energy bar and chew on it without offering him any. I know it is a red flag for him. Even in hostile periods after showdowns, he is always a gentleman first, like offering me this stick he scavenged on the way up for my use as a hiking pole. But if I have travelled this far on the road to being the ultimate bitch, I might as well live it up.

The view is spectacular though. At any other time, I would have taken a few selfies to be posted on social media afterwards. The clouds seem to get darker by the second. I sense him struggling to accept the mistake in navigation and beat a retreat.

"Anyway, since we are here, we might as well spend some time and take in the views." I swing my arms in exaggerated enthusiasm.

"Let's head back. We might still be able to catch up with others," he growls, without taking his eyes off the horizon.

That's the man he has become. Doing the exact opposite of whatever I suggest, and being hopelessly vain. I am pretty sure we were the last ones in the disjointed line of trekkers and we have walked for at least half an hour on the wrong side of the fork. There is no way we can catch up with others.

"No, I think I am going to rest here for a while." I dump my backpack onto the ground and slump on a protruding boulder.

His ears grow red. For a second, I fear he might just leave me and head back to the fork. Instead, he picks up a stone, tosses it, catches it, and repeats. Rolling it on his palm, he drawls, "It might rain, you never know."

I am beginning to enjoy this. He is not exactly begging me to follow him, but he isn't leaving me behind either. I lie down on the outgrowth of the boulder.

"That's okay. It won't be the worst thing to happen."

I dare him to say something he would regret, again, so that I can prove how unreasonable he can be, once and for all. But he hurls the stone across the chasm and stays silent. Minutes crawl by. Then something else crawls up.

A rock python!

I grew up close to the forests, so spotting a snake once in a while was not new to me, though this one looks endless as it slithers close. A chill runs down my spine as its slit eyes stare into mine. Maybe I have willed it to come, as I have likened my existence to being worse than crushed by a python.

It moves closer. I freeze. My mind goes blank.

Suddenly, the stick in my hand is snatched away and wedged between me and the python's path. The python changes its direction, speeds across, and disappears in the undergrowth by the side of the trail. I am in the arms of the man who chose to put himself between me and the python. It must have been terrifying for him as he has never lived anywhere but the city.

"You should have just let it get me." I whimper.

His hands are cold and his heart is thumping.

"Yes, maybe I should have. But…we still have to get back to that fork."

I hate that he still doesn't say how much he loves me or he's sorry to have hurt me. But I am glad to be alive to fight on another day and prove my point. I pick up my backpack, leave the stick, and tread beside him.

The Girl with the Red Umbrella – Anne-Marie Kofoed

(Genre: Drama)

It wasn't raining. The red umbrella swished open with a pop, wellies trudging through the sand. Seagulls screeched above the waters.

When Millie reached the wooden dock, she began counting the planks, "One, two, three…" Her voice was an indistinct murmur. "…thirty, thirty-one, thirty-two, thirty… oh." Gingerly she stepped over the broken plank, mumbling, "Need to let someone know, someone might get hurt, that's no good." A new number followed each step until she reached 97. "Three more and we could have had an even hundred."

The wind picked up, so she clasped her hand tighter around her umbrella - a gift from Gran. "Won't lose you." Her eyes scanned the horizon. "Maybe today they'll come back, one can only dream." Hope never crossed her heart these days; hope was long since lost, taken by the swirling winds that had sailed them away.

Time was never important while dreaming, so she planted her feet at the end of the dock and focused on the narrow line of silver dividing the heavens from the ocean.

A new ship sailed towards the small village, and she bounced on the spot, her toes curling in the yellow wellies. Excitement spread in every part of her soul. But it was never their ship.

"Miss you, Momma, Daddy." She blinked away the tears.

Millie could hear joyful shouts from the ship, its tall mast swaying over the lapping waves. People on the dock helped secure the ship while the crew regaled whoever wanted to listen about their adventure.

"Millie!" The shout was frantic, and when she turned on her heel, the old harbor master, Mr Wally, was waving his arms in the air, beckoning her to return to the beach.

With a sigh Millie moved forward, making a small jump over the cracked number thirty-three plank. "Need to tell Mr Wally." Her pace sped up, and she yelled, "The number thirty-three plank needs to be fixed, Mr Wally." Her free hand waved behind her. "Someone could get hurt."

"What?"

"There's a broken plank."

"Oh, I know, don't worry, Miss Millie, we'll get it fixed. In time." His weathered face wrinkled in a smile, and then everything about him crumbled into a sorrow-filled expression. "Somethin' happened at your Gran's place."

"What?"

"There's an ambulance called."

"Ambulance…" Her tongue stuck to the roof of her mouth, and a small cry slipped over her lips as she plowed through the sand. Leaping over the small stone dike, she found her way back to the little white house with the dilapidated thatched roof. She ignored the fence posts flashing by her; there was no time to count them today.

The red umbrella blew carelessly behind her, her fingers gripping the handle, but she paid no mind to the gusts of wind trying to flip the umbrella inside out.

"I need you to be okay… I need you to be okay!" The words tumbled out of her mouth in an endless plea to whoever would listen. As she skidded to a halt in front of the tiny house, she took a deep breath. The land officer, Mr Johnson, sat outside on Gran's rickety wicker chair, and when he spotted her, he rushed forward, meeting her at the gate.

"Millie, something happened to…"

"Where's Gran?"

"I'm sorry, the paramedics couldn't save her, they said it's her heart."

"No!" Grief tore through her soul mercilessly, splintering her last fragment of dreams. Her heart hammered in her chest.

"I'm sorry…"

"Where is she?" she cut him off, not caring if he was the law. All she wanted was to see her Gran's grey eyes laughing at the squirrels fighting over the breadcrumbs out in the backyard.

Millie's wellies were stuck beside the first stepping stone leading to the front door. Fifteen more until she would find the answer. Taking the first step, she began counting. "One, two, three…" Her eyes blurred with tears as she took each step. "…fourteen, fifteen."

"Perhaps I should see if you can come in." Officer Johnson tapped her shoulder as if she would step aside to let him in.

"No!" Millie pushed forward, and in her haste, she'd forgotten all about the umbrella, which got stuck in the door frame. A snap sounded as the wires bent backward, curling around the red fabric. Something cracked inside her as she took in the damage. "Oh dear, what will Gran say."

"Let me take that for you." Officer Johnson said calmly and reached out for the broken umbrella.

"No." With shaking hands, Millie curled the umbrella wires back where they belonged, but several of them were still twisted. "What will Gran say." Millie swallowed the sob in her throat as she smoothed her hand over the folded umbrella; it was uneven now, the wires stuck out in odd angles under the soft red fabric.

"Are you Mrs Brown's granddaughter?" someone asked.

"She is." Johnson supplied gently, turning Millie around to face the paramedics. "Think she is a bit shaken."

"Gran?" Millie stumbled forward, forgetting all about counting the twenty tiles she would cross over before she reached the bedroom. The paramedics stepped back, all with solemn faces, but still showing the usual sympathetic looks in their eyes. *There goes Millie the Silly, with her special mind, counting stones, fence posts, and heartbeats.* Right now it seemed as if her heart stood still as she stepped over the threshold. It was dark and someone had already opened the window. The scent of roses wafted around her; Gran loved her roses. Bile lodged in her throat as she cried out, "Gran." She slipped closer, the lines crisscrossing the carpet all but forgotten.

Gran's sunken-in, unnaturally grey face stood in stark contrast to her bright red pillowcase. Red was Gran's favorite color. Millie pressed the broken umbrella close to her chest as if to stop her own heart from breaking too. Her fingers tapped over the twisted wires: "One, two, three, four, five, six, seven, eight." All accounted for.

The Kite – Anne-Marie Kofoed

(Genre: Drama)

Melvin reaches for another branch. He hoists himself higher.

"Those spaghetti arms won't help you," Ricky shouts from below; the group around him collapses in a fit of laughter.

Just one more branch and the kite is within reach; Melvin's fingers grasp the torn paper, freeing it, and aim it at the ground.

He looks down and sees the boys leap around the kite. Ricky's boot breaks the sticks. "You're a fool, Melvin."

The shout stabs Melvin's heart and tears trickle down his face.

"Why did I even try?" Melvin whispers as he slips down the tree.

The Last Fete in Steeple Morden – J.I. Mumford

(Genre: Sci-Fi)

Some time ago, in a sweaty, ugly town called Steeple Morden, a dance competition was held as part of the local fete. Among the most popular acts was a skinny lad whose jerking movements—in imitation of a dancing robot—had the town's youth in fits of laughter. The elders, as the music was not too loud, nodded in appreciative silence.

As the applause thinned, a big-city visitor stood up and clapped his hands once. "Give me a half-hour and I'll show you exactly how a 'robot' can dance," he bellowed. Taking the stunned silence as agreement, the visitor marched from the hall and passed out of sight to the edge of the commons. With that, and a chortle from the town baker, the dance competition continued.

Mid-way through the Hoon twins' "Spandex Spandau Ballet"—which only the partially sighted dared watch—the church hall door smashed open.

A booming voice from beyond the door announced, "Presenting LORRRRRRRMAX!"

The music skipped, then silenced. The lights lowered, and the Hoon twins, with frozen smiles and their jazz hands held high, slid sideways from the stage.

The visitor strutted in with a small metal-clad marionette tied to both his fingers and a makeshift T-bar.

When he stepped onto the stage floor, lights focused on him, and a disjointed tune played. The visitor shuffled. Then he slid sideways with the music. He shimmied and even managed a forward roll in concert with his miniature metal heart-shaped mockery of a metal man. The music bellowed and thrummed and shook the halls with a metallic beat. The elders covered their ears, and the youths stared in shock at the performance.

The music ended with a flourish, accompanied with a 720-degree twist flip by the visitor and his metal marionette.

However, the visitor's enthusiasm outclassed the stage's baptismal pool cover. The odd man fell through. The metal marionette strained against the connecting cords and braced itself under its own power.

The locals, who had only just started using cable television, had never seen a real robot in person. The parson fainted. Ava Hoon, the closest of the twins—through fear of the unknown, or merely anger from being upstaged— kicked the struggling metal figure away from the hatch.

It squeaked as it spun across the floor. Its arc defined by the strings. It rolled and twisted in a most odd manner.

The metal man stood. It yanked at the threads around each limb, breaking them easily, one by one. It reached up and removed a tiny helmet. Looking up at the twins, the little technonaught fixed a wide grin. The combination of his impish size and a mouth that nearly circumnavigated his head was not entirely pleasant to look upon.

The twins grimaced. The Parson's wife fainted.

Sirens screamed from the pool. They warned of weapons systems active and armed. The tiny heart-shaped metal clad creature raised his jazz hands and tip-tapped his way to the other side of the stage.

That was the last fete in Steeple Morden.

The Last Word – Thom Brodkin

(Genre: Drama)

I was thirteen when I first met Jason. At the time, I thought Asperger's was the punchline of a defecation joke and being on the spectrum was Roy G. Biv from art class. I doubt anyone else was as happy as I was when he joined our homeroom. In an instant, I was no longer the weirdest kid.

For those unfamiliar with Asperger's, it's a condition where people struggle to show emotion and are uncomfortable making eye contact. Jason had difficulty with both, but that wasn't what set him apart. You see, Jason loved words. He loved the long, melodic, multisyllabic ones best. Why use one boring word when ten glorious ones would be so much better? A shirt wasn't black to him it was, and I quote, The color of night just before dawn. It was Jason who introduced me to words like kaleidoscopical, extravaganza, and my personal favorite onomatopoeia.

At first, I joined the crowd in making fun of Jason. Calling him a freak made me less self-conscious about my greasy hair, zitty face, and Coke-bottle glasses. It's a miracle we became friends. People with Asperger's don't trust others easily, and when they do, they almost never choose assholes like me.

But it turned out we had one thing in common: belting out show tunes. I liked them because my mom did, and he loved them because of all the wonderful words.

When you get home tonight, google Modern Major-General from The Pirates of Penzance. It's filled with beautiful words masterfully strung together, and it was what

I was singing in the school bathroom when Jason walked in and joined me in perfect harmony. I could carry a tune, but Jason, on a sound stage surrounded by urinals, stole the show. We became friends that day, right there in the porcelain conservatory, conveniently located between ignorance and apathy. And, not long after that, the two strangest boys in school somehow became popular. Our singing elicited smiles, even from Jason every now and then.

We finished high school and ended up being roommates in college. I was the one he chose to introduce him the night he gave his speech about Asperger's, and he was the best man at my wedding. My oldest son, Jason, is right there in the front row.

We never thought about death as kids or even as we became adults, so I wasn't prepared when I got the call. His mom said the day would be a little less sad if I gave the eulogy, but I wasn't sure exactly what I would say. I'd say he was a good man and I'll miss him, but for Jason that isn't nearly enough words. You see, he was a spectacular, magnificent, glorious, delightful, wondrous, once-in-a-generation, unbelievably unique, immensely brilliant wordsmith. He was a tremendously talented, gifted, accomplished, first-rate, pitch-perfect, Broadway-quality singer, and I will forever and ever, and even a day past then, longingly miss the very best friend I've ever had.

The Late Late Bartholomew Jones – Thom Brodkin

(Genre: Drama)

You were late the day you were born and on your first day of school.

You were a late talker and loved to stay up late.

The day she told you she was late was the best day of your life. The day she passed, the worst.

She said you'd be late on this day too, and the clock proved her right.

The pastor had already started the eulogy when you spirited down the aisle, turned and bowed like a thespian, then floated into the casket.

You were late but she was waiting for you, and that made all the difference.

The Motorway Daredevil – Alexis Araneta

(Genre: Action/Adventure)

"Life is a motorway. It stretches to infinity if you dare ride in the fast lane," you told her when you dragged her to your black Ducati and strapped her in for a ride. She screamed in protest behind you as you zoomed on the blackened asphalt, the lights streaming red.

As the motor growled, your heart thumped along with the vibrations of the black leather seat. Adrenaline coursed in your veins as you sped past metal signs and the gust tousled your long blonde tresses.

As the motor growled, her heart palpitated along with the vibrations of the black leather seat. Adrenaline pumped in her veins as metal signs got closer and closer and the gust slapped her across her delicate face.

Your face broke into a mischievous grin as you removed your meaty hands from the handlebars whilst accelerating. You let the motorbike drift in zigzag lines as you chased the rush of excitement inside you.

Her face froze into a horrified grimace as she clung on to your muscular body whilst you accelerated. Her heart beat in zigzag lines as it chased the shock of panic inside her.

"Life is a motorway; make sure neither you nor those around you exit too early," you realised as you wrenched the handlebars of your black Ducati and came on the path of a large lorry. She screamed in terror behind you as you both skidded on the blackened asphalt, both of your blood streaming red.

The Play's the Thing – Deidra Whitt Lovegren

(Genre: Comedy)

It is ungodly hot and Hamlet should shut up.

"You cannot call it love, for at your age the heyday in the blood is tame," overenunciates one of the actors, holding a plastic skull. The skull does not appear until Act 5, and Hamlet is certainly not waving it at his mother while lecturing her on her sex life.

The community theater auditions are going poorly.

"Next!"

"You may want to pay close attention to the next one," warns Bob, handing me another actor's resume. It's so humid inside the moldy theater that the paper curls.

Bob and I are old friends, finding ourselves surprisingly single at 60. How he convinces me to help him stage *Hamlet* in the middle of the hottest July on record chiefly results from my utter boredom. Retirement is turning out to be stupefying, as there are only so many crossword puzzles one can do.

"Why am I considering this actress more than the others? It says here she's almost our age, Bob, and she's auditioning for *Ophelia*?"

"She owns five KFC franchises," Bob replies.

"So Ophelia is going to drown in hydrogenated soybean oil?"

"This woman can finance a large part of the production. The city only contributes so much, and I'm not good at fundraising. Do you want to shake down a few car dealerships to support the arts?"

I skeptically peruse her resume.

"C'mon, Bob. She's just played Annie. *It's a half-lived life for us.* Are you sure the Queen of Fried Chicken is right for our production? How about we start a GoFundMe page instead?"

"How about you look at our Ophelia," Bob suggests, motioning towards the stage.

"Fine," I sulk.

I hear her before I see her.

Her footsteps are not the tentative taps of a poor, dutiful Ophelia, but long purposeful strides of the King of Denmark. She is tall with unruly hair, dark brown eyes staring down at Bob and I as if we were auditioning for her.

"I have rehearsed Act 3 Scene 1," she says.

"Come again—?" I flip through the papers in front of me. *She's gorgeous.*

She waits for us, suffering fools gladly. "I will need one of you to read Hamlet's part."

"Me. I'll do it." I volunteer while sweat pools under my armpits. I will kill Bob if he offers otherwise. *I want her to talk with me.*

"Ready?" she inquires with an arched eyebrow. *O, that I might kiss that eyebrow!*

"I am absolutely ready."

Bob audibly snickers, and I hate him for knowing me so well.

She pauses, collecting all the kinetic energy in the rundown auditorium.

"My lord, I have love-tokens of yours to return to you," she laments, a heartbroken maiden.

Her transformation blinds me. I cannot find my place on the page. Bob threatens to roar with laughter at my besotted state, but, thankfully, he controls himself enough to point out my line.

"No, not I. I never gave you anything!" I stand, calling out to her.

"My honored lord, you know right well you did." She eloquently articulates each syllable. I sit down because I don't trust my knees.

"Are you virtuous?" I ask. *Please say no.*

"My lord?"

"Are you fair?" *She grows more beautiful the longer I look at her. I cannot stop looking at her.*

"What means your lordship?"

"I did love you once," I proclaim, more ardently than the script calls for.

Bob pointedly stares at me. I punch him under the table.

"Indeed, my lord, you made me believe so." Ophelia is all vulnerability, eyes wider than the sea.

Due to the heat, her eyeliner has smudged, making her look desperate. The next lines are cruel, and I read them poorly because they are not true.

"You should have not believed me. I loved you not."

The actress appears as if physically in pain. In a dejected voice, she simply states: "I was the more deceived."

I rip out my own heart by mumbling the words, "Get thee to a nunnery."

Bob applauds while she formally bows, smiling from ear to ear. As she gathers her things, I sit paralyzed, as I've just fallen in love with a woman who trafficks in mashed potatoes.

To my delight and disbelief, I watch her make her way towards us.

"So, how are the auditions coming along?" she fishes.

"Very good. Lots of talent," Bob offers in his noncommittal way.

"Well, we haven't seen *that* much talent," I add. "But you were excellent. What I mean is that you read the part in a talented way. We saw your talent." *Kill me.*

She views us skeptically.

"Well, let me know if I get the part. If I do, I'll have to hire another manager or two."

"They say the owl was a baker's daughter!" I blurt out one of Ophelia's nonsensical lines, making a jaunty gesture to further embarrass myself.

"We know what we are, but know not what we may be," she replies over her shoulder, and my heart nearly bursts. She turns on her high heels to leave.

After the auditions, Bob and I walk out into the evening air, stifling hot, beads of sweat trickling down our faces.

"I think we have a solid cast," he says. He dabs his face

with his tie.

"Hamlet is a little weak," I caution him, but it would be hard to find an equal to Ophelia's stage presence. *And her eyes.*

"Do you want to grab dinner?"

"No, I have other plans," I casually reply.

"Are these plans original or extra crispy?"

I place my hand over my heart. "Do not take tenders for true pay, which are not sterling. Tender yourself more dearly, Bob."

"That's what you're going with? Chicken tender puns?" Bob rolls his eyes.

"You'll tender me a fool," I say, blowing Bob a stage kiss.

And then I do what Hamlet should have done.

I walk to my car, determined to find the fair Ophelia at one of five KFC locations.

The Red Field – Daniel R. Hayes

(Genre: Horror)

"I hope the leaf carcasses serve their purpose," Todd Riley said, plugging his blood-soaked shovel into the ground. "In time, the body will rot and become one with this festering field."

"What are you doing out here?"

Todd scornfully whipped his head around and saw Mary wearing a blue bathrobe. Her pink curlers were steaming in the cool morning dew. "Mind your business," he gruffed.

"Why don't you mind yours!" she replied. "We've only been dating a few days, and you want to talk to me like that. You should be ashamed of yourself!"

"Shame is for witless scoundrels," Todd said, taking in the barren field that covered his 100-acre farm. "A real man takes pride tending his land."

"So, which are you?"

"I'm not in the mood for sarcasm. Can't you see this field needs some love and tenderness? I've been working all summer, but no matter what I do, nothing grows. A shadow lingers above and hides the sun. I'm at my wit's end."

"Oh, why do I bother?"

"I wonder that myself," Todd said, wiping the sweat beads from his rugged brow.

Mary ignored the wry remark and asked, "Have you tried watering it? I don't know much about planting, but it hasn't rained here for several months."

"Yes," Todd snapped. "I have sprinklers set up to go off every morning and evening. A good farmer would be stupid if he didn't know that!"

"Hmm…that's what I thought," Mary scoffed. "What were you burying there?"

"Why are you so curious all of a sudden? When you delivered that package to my door a few days ago, and I asked you out, I had no idea you would turn out to be such a busybody!"

Mary waved her hands across her curves and said, "Well, I do have a body that stays busy, so I will take that as a compliment. I must be crazy for sticking around."

"You know where the door is."

"For crying out loud, Todd, I don't live here! I was only asking a question!"

"Fine! If you must know, I buried something…special… that I think will help the field grow. I use the dead leaves to coax the ground like fertilizer, which is an old trick my daddy taught me a long time ago. Oh, how disappointed he would have been to see these fields empty."

Mary looked at the cracked soil and shook her head. "How long have you been a farmer? You don't seem to be very good at it."

Todd pulled his brown trousers up and frowned. "I've been a farmer since I was a kid. So, I'd say about forty years. Usually, a man's hard work pays off in the harvest he sows, and Lord knows I've been breaking my back every day. I just need a bit of luck to get me through this rough spot."

"I think you need more than luck, old man!"

"Keep your opinions to yourself. I don't have time for all this bickering."

As Todd turned his back from Mary, she saw the red splatter on the tip of his shovel. She crossed her arms and nudged him out of the way.

"Hey, what are you doing?"

Mary kicked the leaves away with her white sneakers and saw a pale gray hand protruding from the rotting soil. That would have scared the Dickens out of anyone else, but the fact that this hand had three elongated fingers was another story.

"I knew you killed him!"

"What?!" Todd spat. "You know what this thing is?"

"He was my husband! Of course, I know what he was!"

Todd held his tongue as his mind raced with endless possibilities that seemed implausible.

Mary wiped away her tears and gave Todd a look that would have killed any sane man. She plunged her fingers into her curvy hips and ripped the façade away. There was no blood, only a rubbery plastic that concealed her true form.

As Todd gazed upon Mary's lanky body, gray skin, and huge black bulbous eyes, he knew she wasn't from this world. "What are you?" he finally said.

"We are the Druvoix, and my true name is Vrudu," she explained coldly. "We are alien researchers from the planet Rudon surveying Earth for potential expansion of our species."

"I-I don't understand," Todd stuttered.

"I know you don't. You humans are not very bright compared to our high intellect. You especially seem to be bordering on what we would call intelligent life. My husband, Gruba, surveyed your land and concluded it would serve as a great nesting ground for our seedlings. When he went missing a few days ago, I concealed my true form to discover what happened. Now I know you killed him."

"You're dang right, I killed him," Todd admitted. "When I found him sneaking around this field, I smacked him with this shovel, and he went down faster than a bag of bricks. He never saw me coming! I decided to bury him here, hoping the soil would drink his nutrients and bring some much-needed life back to the ground."

"Well," Vrudu huffed. "Maybe you're not as dumb as I thought you were."

"That's it!" Todd yelled. "I'm not taking your insults anymore!"

He swung the shovel at Vrudu's oval-shaped skull, but she grabbed the wooden handle before his attack could come to fruition.

She yanked the gardening tool away and said, "Not this time, Todd!"

Whack!

The impact left a crater the size of a bowling ball on Todd's forehead. He fell like a dead tree, for that's all he was to Vrudu.

Suddenly, the shade covering the field moved, and Vrudu's invisible ship became visible. It consumed Todd's limp body in a blinding light. After a low grumble, the cylindrical, silver spaceship sprayed the field with red blood and green ichor.

Vrudu stepped aside with a smile and said, "Soon, this unfertile soil will give birth to our seeds. The first step to colonizing this planet is complete."

The Sapieneria – Jon Casper

(Genre: Drama)

Properly prepared, human skin was as crispy and bubbly as crackling, but the chops were never as succulent as pork tenderloin. Then again, Harlan glamorized his memory of backyard barbecue in times long past, so he couldn't be sure.

He and Knut reached for the last rib, but Knut was faster.

"It's a pity." Knut gnawed flesh from bone, grease glistening in his ducktail beard. "Pigs are pork, cows are beef. This needs a name."

"Bakolo." The word came from the far corner. The friends swiveled their necks to meet two pairs of eyes.

A clean-cut, thirtyish man sat in a booth, his severe stare unwavering. Before him, a juvenile pig hunched on the tabletop, softly grunting.

The man raked fingers through his upswept, tawny hair as he approached. "Actually, very few animals have separate words for their meat, but bakolo is what cannibals in Fiji called … well …"

"People?" Knut sucked sauce from a fingertip.

"Prey." The stranger stuck out his hand. "Name's Sigmund. First time at a Sapieneria?"

Harlan and Knut exchanged a glance, then shook the man's hand.

"Cerberus loves 'em." Sigmund thumbed toward his pet pig. "Then again, she'll eat anything."

Harlan gaped at the poetic justice. "You feed your pig …

human meat?"

"Bakolo, yes." Sigmund grinned. "She's doing her part. The population's already dropped to early millennium numbers, with six months left in the harvest. At this rate, we'll reach pre-Industrial Revolution levels."

Knut scoffed. "Sociologists predict equilibrium before then."

"Yeah, right." Sigmund wedged himself onto the bench beside Knut. "Veggie burgers aren't going to cut it, now that folks got a taste for it." He waved at the pile of bones, picked-clean. "Come January, we're supposed to go back to lab-grown meat? Fried bugs?" He wrinkled his nose. "No, thank you."

"They'll lock you up," said Knut, tossing in the last bare bone.

Sigmund folded his arms. "Only if they catch me."

Cerberus squealed plaintively from the corner table. Sigmund rushed to cradle her, caressing her floppy ears. "Can you believe people used to eat these furbabies? Barbaric!"

Harlan withheld the many times he'd consumed Cerberus's ancestry as a boy.

Sigmund paced before the smoldering sunset outside the diner's full-height windows. "At least with bakolo there's implicit justice: man versus man. Beyond culling the population, we're satisfying our natural blood-thirst. It's therapeutic! The bonus? Billions fewer carbon footprints!"

Knut cleared his throat. "So, have you ever …?"

"Killed a man?" Sigmund brightened. "You bet! Not to

eat, though. The juicy ones are too easy. The competitive ones are tough, like jerky. The Purina plant gives me two grand per head for the inedible ones. Apparently, dogs *love* bakolo."

Harlan caught Knut's gaze and nodded.

Knut closed the distance to his quarry in a single bound. Ochre sunlight glinted on his carbon steel blade as it glided across Sigmund's neck. The man collapsed, his beloved pet lapping at ribbons of blood.

"C'mon," said Knut. "Let's get him into the kitchen."

The Storm – Anne-Marie Kofoed

(Genre: Historical Fiction)

The squally winds slice over the frayed sails, and the canvas rips even more. Captain Blackeye stomps across the rough planks of the deck on his wooden leg. He looks to the heavens and curses the winds of fate. The bloody storm ruined his treasured ship.

A whimper echoes through the fog; he turns around. The boy looks up at him with haunted eyes, blinking in fear. Eyes mirroring his soul. Captain Blackeye reaches out and notices his white bony fingers, devoid of flesh and muscle. He clasps his chest and feels no heartbeat. The bloody storm was his demise.

The Tea Party – Robert Burns

(Genre: Drama)

The tea party was perfect. Tiny teacups set upon tiny saucers. Tiny cakes. Porcelain teapot upon a lace doily.

"More chamomile, Mr. Bear?" Sallie asked teddy—always her favorite—pouring pretend tea into his cup. "Mrs. Grey?" she politely offered the stuffed goose.

"Sallie? Time to go," Mother called.

"Coming," the little one said, watching the tea party dissolve as she stepped through the door, rejoining the bleak reality of the sharecropper's shack.

Mother fixed her black veil. "Daddy's waiting."

Hand in hand, they stepped out into dusty sunlight. Sallie squinted over her shoulder and whispered goodbye to her childhood.

The Ways of Our People – Hannah P. Simmons

(Genre: Drama)

When Great Grandmother died, we all came together, because that is what family does. We all gathered at the house of her daughter, my Nana. The women cooked food in the kitchen, the children played in the yard, and the men sat together and talked. We sang songs on the porch, while Father played the guitar. We held her pictures in dollar store frames. And we embraced, and smiled, and shared, and grieved. Because that is our way.

When Great Grandmother died, we all came together, because that is what family does. And I looked at my Aunts and their husbands. I looked at Father and Sister and the cousins. I looked longingly at their black hair and darkened skin. At their raised cheekbones and deep brown eyes that seemed to disappear when they smiled. I looked with jealousy at the traces of heritage that danced across their faces. And though I knew the blood of the tribe flowed also through my veins, I was not the same.

Mother's people had come from across the water, not many years ago. Father's people had been here since before. They'd lived here when time was not kept. When the passing of a day had been measured by the path of the sun crossing to sit in the mountains to the west. They were a fierce people. A proud people. A people gifted in hunting and war, but also in dance and stories.

I loved the stories. The story of the first days, of when the Water Beetle dove to the bottom of the endless waters and brought a piece of mud to the surface. Of when the mountains were formed by the wings of the Buzzard as he flew over the soft Earth. Of the trees who were told to keep watch over the new Earth for seven nights, but only the Evergreens stayed awake, and so now they never sleep. The story of the first strawberries, a gift from the Great Spirit to settle a lovers' quarrel. I told the stories to the small children that I often cared for.

I read their histories and committed the names of their chiefs and shamans to memory. I learned the songs they sang in the original tongue. I covered my notebooks with the symbols of their language. I held them close in the spirit pouch that sat in my room, containing small pebbles from the reservation, so that I could carry their land with me no matter where I might go.

But, even so, as I stood there amid my family, my heart ached with the knowledge that no one would ever look at me and know.

When Great Grandmother died, her son came. I had never met Uncle before. But I knew him when I saw him. I had been told his hair would be in braids. That he would wear necklaces made by the women of the tribe. That he often sat by council fires and spoke with the chiefs.

When Great Grandmother died, we all came together, because that is what family does. We all gathered at the house of her daughter, my Nana. And as Uncle came into the house, the grandchildren all greeted him. And as we crowded around him in the doorway, he asked, "Which one has learned the ways of our people?"

Nana spoke, and I heard my name.

Without hesitation, Uncle pulled the tribal feather from

his hair, wound in a leather cord, and placed it in my hands. I stood there with my blonde hair and green eyes and the pride of our ancestors pulsing through me.

That day, as I carefully tied Uncle's feather into my own braid, I vowed to keep them alive. In my stories. In my songs. In so many little ways.

The Weaver of Losdale – C.P. Misola

(Genre: Fantasy)

Nestled in a dell surrounded by woodland, the village of Losdale settles in for the night as its Weaver sits at his desk, waiting. David's tea grows tepid, and his weapon for the evening — a book titled *Charlotte's Web* — lays ready. He knows in his bones, after the hullabaloo of the day, his weaving will be required.

Damn Old Joshua and his lamentations on the state of his cows. He's unsettled the entire village.

"The Wood provides, and the Weaver sustains," Agatha whispers into David's mind, intruding on his huff.

"The Wood provides because you ask it to, Agatha."

She called herself the Village Hag. But to the villagers, she was known as the Walker. A cruel title now that she is a mere skull sitting on his desk.

Knocks at his door chase away the memory of her cackle. As expected, it is the young milkmaid, Alice, come on behalf of Old Joshua with tears streaming down her face. David recalls the day he first came upon Alice sprawled on the Lane, distraught, disoriented and crawling away from Wisp Wood with a face-full of snot and tears. It took him days to weave peace into her. He started with *Anne of Green Gables* and almost gave up with *Little House on the Prairie*, but he found her calm in *Charlotte's Web*. It was then that David decided it would suit her to be cared for by the village farmer, who had once shared her now-forgotten pain.

"Come, child. Old Joshua is in need of my weaving."

They hurry through the village — past the home of the baker driven to self harm at the loss of her child.

Past the home of the pig farmer, bullied to despair.

Past the lady with the chicken coop, who never found her place in the world beyond the woods.

Until they finally arrive at Old Joshua's bedside, the farmer who was beaten as a child, only to find him whimpering the words that alarmed the village throughout the day.

"The cows! The cows!"

Starting at the last chapter seems prudent — David finds his place and allows his voice to take on the timbre of the Weaver.

The Weaver sustains, the Weaver brings peace; the Weaver takes so they will never remember.

David leaves Old Joshua's homestead with heavy feet and a throbbing headache. He left Alice breathing deep and even, immersed in dreamless rest whilst Old Joshua drew shallow gasps. Gasps that David expects will soon turn into death rattles. But death cannot be woven away, and the old farmer's imminent passing is expected. It's the cows that weigh heavily on David's mind. *Sick cows, practically emaciated. Why?* He cannot begin to fathom, and yet, deep in his bones, he knows, if left unchecked, it will spread to the chickens, then to the pigs. *Soon the villagers of Losdale shall starve.*

He returns to his desk and partakes of his now cold tea. The infused lavender, grown in his own backyard, has grown bitter and does little to calm his mind. This was Agatha's realm, not his. Once, she would have only needed to walk up the Lane and Wisp Wood would have opened for her, as it did when it brought new villagers. It would have welcomed her into its depths and she would have walked amongst its moss covered oak, between the stunted and twisted branches. Through Agatha, Wisp Wood would know, and it would provide.

"It is not unheard of," she said on her deathbed, "for Walkers to perish before their replacement is found — we are a rare breed. Your Walker will come, David. Until then, you must endure. Losdale must have its Weaver."

Agatha left macabre instructions that led to her skull's presence on David's desk — his last connection to Wisp Wood and his sole beacon to his Walker.

The first time he used the skull was to request a healer after Old Joshua took to his bed ill. The second time was when the healer informed him that Old Joshua would not last, and Wisp Wood gave him Alice. Each plea cracked Agatha's skull, and with the skull's delicate state, David grew to fear that his next request would be his last.

"The cows are sick, Agatha. Soon the rest of the livestock will follow. But if you break, what is to become of my Walker? My villagers are aging, and Wisp Wood requires a Walker to know what the village lacks."

"The Wood provides…"

David waves away Agatha's reply. Resolute, he fills his mind only with the thought of a veterinarian — a foreign word he vaguely remembers from his time in the world beyond.

Agatha's skull shatters and becomes dust beneath his palm.

At dawn, David finds a man unconscious on the Lane in front of his cottage.

The Wood provides.

The first weaving is the most difficult — it requires the right book. David delves into the man's mind and sees his pain, so similar to that of Alice and Old Joshua. Opting for *Charlotte's Web*, he begins to unravel the man's — Ian's — life. He safeguards Ian's knowledge of animal healing. He plucks away the day Ian's father shot the family dog in a fit of drunken rage, takes every ounce of guilt Ian suffered after putting one of his patients down, and weaves it into the fiber of the book. In its place he weaves Old Joshua's knowledge of his farm, his cows, Alice, and the village.

By nightfall, Old Joshua is buried and Ian sleeps soundly in his stead. David finds himself at the end of the Lane, sprinkling the last of Agatha's ashes, watching as the wind carries her into Wisp Wood. *The cows are safe — Ian will see to them. But at what cost? What is to become of Losdale without its Walker?*

"The Wood provides, and the Weaver sustains."

Two – James Lynch

(Genre: Suspense)

I never expected that the last thing I would ever see would be his face. I gave it a lot of thought, more than most I would guess, but his pale, craggy face with its gray eyes and dense, graying hair was not on my list.

Moments earlier all I could see was the sky, a shimmering flawless blue spangled with gold in one eye and smeared with dusk in the other. I was content with that; it was peaceful, poetic, twilight above me as my night fell. And then his face appeared like an afternoon moon, faint and ephemeral, sneering through his bushy beard, drawing closer every time I drew a breath that I thought would be the last, until he was so close, he obscured everything else.

I smell old coffee and licorice. The wrinkles on his forehead remind me of rippled sand on a pristine beach. I am suddenly struck by the fact that I have never been so close to him. His eyes, deeply set within shadowed canyons separated by the smooth ridge of his nose, look tired.

His tongue slides out and moistens his lips before they part, revealing his teeth – my God, his teeth are perfect – and allowing a lonely chuckle to escape.

"You know," he begins in his familiar voice, all gravel and oil, "it was always going to end this way. It was inevitable."

I hate you; the words cannot escape my brain.

"Now, now, don't try to talk. Nothing you could say would surprise me." An uncovered cough makes him pause; his sickly saccharine breath makes my eyes tear. He shakes his head and looks away. "Does it hurt much? I would imagine it does. You're quite a mess. Would you like me to describe it to you?"

No. I still cannot speak, so I close my eyes and force every bit of strength I can find into moving my head. He is looking away when I open them again. Did he see? Did I even move?

"No, I wouldn't either. It's quite gruesome. Honestly, I'm amazed you are still alive." He faces me again – the edges of my vision have darkened, framing him in a penumbra of my ebbing existence. "There's not much time left, and we have come so far. Despite everything, I feel like there is still much left to say. I don't expect you can say anything. So please, allow me."

He vanishes from my sight; I pray that this next breath will be the end, while the bruised gold sky is all I can see. I cannot even feel my own breathing, so perhaps I am already dead and this . . . encounter . . . is just my brain filling my last moments with random bits of flotsam. I wonder why my mind conjured him instead of Emma.

He reappears with a sigh, that creased, weathered face now at an odd angle in my vision. One side of his mouth crinkles in a smile. "Oh, you're thinking about Emma, aren't you? I can always tell. Your face softens ever so slightly when you do. It makes sense that you would think about her now; your help was rarely welcome, and when it was you were never able to be there." What little pleasantness was there is replaced with sardonic glee. "But don't worry about her. I will take loving care of her once you're gone. Better care, in fact, than you ever did."

Even now, at the waning verges of life, I know my face has flushed; the heat is barely perceptible to me, but his teeth and rough laugh acknowledge the color in my cheeks. "Are you truly angry? I only do the things you could not. That is why I exist, isn't it? To be the person you could never be?"

Somehow, desperately, I spit-whisper, "You. Are not. Me."

He pulls back, stunned I could form the words. He coughs again, a ragged sound that sprinkles warm saliva on my face. I desperately want to wipe it away, but my body will not comply. "I am better than you," he growls, "just as you wanted. I am all the things you could not be, all the things you desperately wanted to be. I am Jekyll to your Hyde, the better half of you." His wild eyebrows angle up, deepening the dunes of his forehead. "Did you honestly think you were the hero of this story? That you were the better of us?"

Fingers of pain grab the back of my eyes and clamp down; everything goes glittery neon white for a lifetime, and when the pain subsides and the world bleeds back into existence, he is gone. Relieved, I try to will Emma to my side. Instead, his tenebrous, sweat-slicked face materializes once more.

He sweeps aside curtains of hair that have fallen in front of his eyes; his dirty fingers brush through my hair as well. "We were never two. Despite all you did to break away from the things you hated about yourself, we were always one. It is not your failure; it is a failing of us all. You could not exist without those things you embodied in me, and I will carry you with me forever. It is our imperfections – our flaws, the things we despise about ourselves – that make us perfect."

My eyelids shudder and close. My final willful act is to

force them open one last time. He is so close, my vision so clouded, all I can see is my reflection in the gray of his eyes. Within the depths of those imperfect circles floats my face – *his* face – pale and stippled with tiny red dots, beard ripped off in patches, so tired and serene as the torn, raw petals of life flutter away. Before my vision fades forever, his eyes widen with surprise. The last things I feel are his head falling onto my chest, his greasy hair itching my lips, and a climactic moment of wholeness.

Two Adjacent Ads – Cindy Strube

(Genre: Comedy)

LOST: Champion canary. Reward.
FOUND: Cat. Black. Well fed. Smug.

Under the Knife ~ A Matter of Perspective – Cindy Strube

(Genre: Drama)

"Great choice, Liv!" Dixie enthused, slathering butter on a roll.

"I know, right? All made from scratch—what's not to like?"

"Good thing you booked an outside table," Dixie said. "More privacy. The chatter from inside feels like a stage set with directions: _Cutlery clinks._" She made a swirl in the butter.

"You're using that knife like an artist creating an oil painting, hon. It's bread. Eat it or I will!" TJ chuckled.

"Speaking of stages and artists…" Liv leaned forward. "What if this—" She gestured with her fork. "What if _all_ this—town, street, bistro, the very _atmosphere_—is a scene painted by an artist? And we're just figures. Or figments."

"Figments made of pigments!" TJ guffawed. Dixie poked him and shook her head slightly. Liv didn't always have a sense of humor.

"I'm serious!" Liv stated. "How do we know it's _not_ a painting? Or a stage backdrop, like Dixie said. Remember Shakespeare? All the world's a stage!"

Carson frowned. "Liv's got a point. See that sign across the street? _Studio Niccolò._ There's a light on inside. Now, suppose the artist is there, painting us, this very moment."

Nick was, in fact, painting them that very moment. Working *at night was a challenge, but the unexpected rain shower added visual interest, reflecting light off wet asphalt. The accompanying humidity was problematic, but nothing he couldn't manage.* I'll just allow extra drying time, *he told himself, adding a spot of butter yellow to the blade of the woman's knife.*

"You don't believe that, do you?" TJ scoffed.

Carson shrugged. "I don't not believe it."

"What about beyond this moment?" Dixie challenged. "Our shared history? We've known each other for years! Our kids grew up together. This hypothetical artist didn't paint all that."

"Ah, but maybe we just believe those memories because the artist gave them to us." Carson turned to his wife. "What do you think, Liv?"

Liv nodded. "Sure. That would explain it."

TJ choked on a crumb and grabbed his goblet. Dixie could see that he was swallowing a retort along with the water. He didn't go for Liv's cosmic ideas.

"More water, sir?" The waiter appeared, carrying a sweating jug.

Nick chose a slim, pointed knife to dab glistening droplets onto the jug. A couple of thin rivulets trickled down the side.

"Eee!" Dixie rubbed her arm where icy water had dripped. The waiter apologized. "Oh, no, it's OK," Dixie said. "Actually, the cool feels good. The humidity is awful tonight, with the heat and rain."

"Pineapple Express," the waiter said. "Air's so thick, you could cut it with a knife."

Nick stepped back to view the whole picture. Needs more vibrant color there. Red shirt. *With a narrow, flat implement, he gently lifted the blue paint away. Everyone jumped up from the table, ruining the scene. Nick threw down his knife in disgust, splattering red paint across the canvas.*

"*Oww!*" Carson gasped, clutching his side. Sticky crimson oozed through a gaping hole in his shirt.

Uncle Merb and the Missing Sock – David McCahan

(Genre: Comedy)

"Tell that Meshuggeneh Seinfeld he still owes me for the socks bit."

My Uncle Merb told me that every time I went out on a job.

Uncle Merb was under the impression that everyone who worked in the entertainment business knew everyone else.

I knew no one. No one famous, anyway.

I was a member of IATSE Local 1, the stagehands union. I worked as a set dresser. Basically a glorified furniture mover. Without the glory.

My family ran a third-generation moving company in Brooklyn. The stagehands gig was more appealing. I was happier coming home each night instead of driving all over the eastern half of the United States.

It was on a move from Bensonhurst to St. Louis that my then Uncle Salvatore became Uncle Merb. The job was supposed to take a week. My uncle was gone four months.

My father thought he'd found a girl. My mother thought he'd found a racket. My Uncle Merb, né Sal, had found religion.

"I found Jewish."

"You what?" my father asked, incredulous, eyeing the yarmulke on his brother's head.

"I found Jewish." Merb repeated.

What he was trying to say was he'd converted to Judaism. Like when people becoming Christian say they found Jesus, Uncle Merb, in his words, "found Jewish". He never ever found political correctness, but he did find Judaism.

As fate would have it, the truck broke down outside a St. Louis synagogue just as services were dismissing for the day.

The members of the congregation jumped right in. They found a mechanic, put Uncle Merb up in one of their homes, fed him, and even arranged for the load to be delivered to its destination.

"I never felt more welcome," he said. As Uncle Sal, he'd been a lapsed Catholic. As a converted Jew, Uncle Merb was devout.

He went to temple, studied Hebrew, of course learning the swear words first. He even insisted on a bris because his secular circumcision as a baby "didn't count."

"What do you mean it don't count?" my father asked, unconsciously crossing his legs.

"Well, it obviously counts, physiologically," Merb's rabbi explained, forcing back a laugh. "But from a religious point of view…"

"From a religious point of view, you gotta cut my brother's schwanz again," my father shouted, gesturing obliquely towards his nether regions.

"In Yiddish, it's actually pronounced schvantz," the rabbi began, trying to make a joke, but seeing my father was finding no humor in it, he quickly assumed a more sober expression. "Yes, yes. For religious purposes."

We were all invited/required to attend along with the

members of Merb's new synagogue.

"The things we do for family," my father grumbled.

The room was half Jews, half Italian Catholics. It was like the set up to one of Uncle Merb's always inappropriate jokes. When the mohel made his cut, fifty percent of the room shouted the customary "Mazel tov!" The other fifty percent shouted "Jesus Christ!"

"Well, there's something you don't hear at a bris everyday," the mohel joked.

Traditionally, this was when the male baby's Hebrew name was revealed. The entire room had the same reaction this time.

"Merb?" almost everyone said at once.

Turns out it was a name he'd spotted glowing one night on an old neon candy store sign.

"Most Jewishest name I ever saw," he said, even though it turned out it was Danish. At least he got to coin a new awkward term with "Jewishest."

"And it looks great up in lights," Merb beamed.

Outside of becoming Jewish, the thing Uncle Merb wanted most was to be famous. A famous comedian, more specifically. Uncle Merb had his funny moments, scattered between the uncomfortable majority. He could make a roomful of relatives ache with laughing, usually after everyone had had plenty to drink. He was situationally funny. He wasn't stand up funny. The couple of times he'd tried an open mic night, he'd bombed. Not that he'd noticed. He'd been too preoccupied laughing at his own material.

Which is how the whole Seinfeld thing came about.

Ever since we were kids, Uncle Merb's biggest and most constant gripe was how he kept losing socks in the wash. It both confused and infuriated him. Over time, he developed a whole conspiracy theory about someone being a sock thief, and it usually skewed towards one of us kids stealing them to masturbate with.

So, when Merb saw the premiere of *Seinfeld*, who up to that point he'd loved because he'd wanted to be supportive of his fellow Jew—a statement that elicited eye rolls from everybody in the family—Merb hit the roof.

"Maniak," Merb shouted, pointing at the TV, which I found out later roughly translated to cocksucker. "Lech timtzotz elef za'een!"—which is essentially the undertaking of a committed Maniak.

"This schlemiel stole my routine!"

"You tell him when you see him," he said to me from that moment on. "You promise."

"I promise, Uncle Merb," I said because the odds of me ever crossing paths with Jerry Seinfeld were about as likely as getting struck by lightning.

Eleven years later, lightning struck.

I wound up on a gig at the Beacon Theater. A Jerry Seinfeld concert. I was alone way up in the rigging above the stage a few hours before the show, and down below me out he walked and out it came.

"Hey Seinfeld, my Uncle Merb says you still owe him for the socks bit," I shouted down, unseen.

He didn't react. No one did. I was relieved. I'd done what I'd promised. I figured that was it.

I was wrong.

Ten minutes later I got fired off the job. And banned from all jobs at the Beacon.

As I was being ushered out, I fired one parting shot.

"Lech timtzotz elef za'een, Seinfeld!"

My Uncle Merb hugged me for the first time in my life when I got home.

"I'm so proud, I could plotz," he said, slapping my cheek.

The things we do for family.

We Make Good Pets – J.I. Mumford

(Genre: Sci-Fi)

"Look TavisHoosh, I trained my hooman to wear cloth and walk like us!"

"Quite remarkable; I've never seen such a thing!" said TavisHoosh. "You must show him off to your gene-mates!"

"I will bring him to the next sharing!"

At the sharing, a feast was held to celebrate a newly hatched TargHoosh. AndussHoosh cleared its throats and announced, "I have taught my hooman to walk like us, after a fashion. And to wear cloth and stand at the nutritional teat without feeding until I unclasp my antero-lateral tentacles!"

"Do share!"

"TavisHoosh, if you please." Attendants brought the human in, and it laid near AndussHoosh's side as if to whisper in his aural mesh. AndussHoosh flashed a pattern near the man's face.

This was the cue to push along the floor; the man pumped his arms to engage his shoulder blades. He circumnavigated the room on his back, settling near where he started.

"Brilliant!" called his gene-mates. "Bravo!"

"How fine he looks covered in a Tag-cloth," added one.

"Another trick!" called another.

A new pattern flashed, and the human rolled to his front, exposing his bare and scarred shoulders. He scurried to the feeding teat, then quickly laid on his side, staring at AndussHoosh.

"Funny how they move; how do they ever balance tilted on their backside?" commented one.

"Such small eye spots; how do they ever see?" said another.

AndussHoosh clasped then un-clasped his sub tentacles, indicating the human could eat. And he did, eagerly.

"I would suppose they are nearly as intelligent as a small, newborn Targhoosh," said TavisHoosh in jest.

"Just a fashionable pet; you'll soon tire of training it," said FiiffulHoosh.

"You're just jealous because yours is so lazy!" said AndussHoosh

"I threw mine out. It kept leaking."

Where Do I Go From Here – Suma Jayachandar

(Genre: Suspense)

The gates look magnificent, out of this world.

You check the time. Perfect. You've arrived fashionably late.

"Child! You're late," a voice booms.

Indignant, you wonder if you should point out you are attending this once-in-a-lifetime event barefoot.

The buckled shoes you wore to school, the ballet shoes you pirouetted in on the stage, the pencil heels you walked down the aisle in, the sneakers you thrust your feet in to watch soccer practices, and the Velcro wides for the diabetic; none of them fitted your now formless feet.

"But I made it, didn't I?"

"Everyone does… eventually. Welcome home, child!"

Where the Light Drowns – Riel Rosehill

(Genre: Horror)

Dex replaced Carl after he'd been stupid enough to drown. It happened three days after we'd left that miserable decompression chamber, and while the rest of us craved to walk on dry land, Carl—like a fish—had gone right back under water, never to swim again.

His body had been retrieved by Dex Turner, the same commercial diver who then took his place. Brand spanking new to saturation diving, young Dex arrived with a big smile, fresh and ready to work on the rig. Full of youthful energy to throw himself into an adventure, he could've taken advantage of it and stayed on the surface to party. Why he chose instead to be sunken six hundred metres deeper than where the dead were buried was unfathomable to me.

'I want to find a mermaid,' he replied when I asked him.

He said it in such an honest manner, it took me a moment to offer a polite laugh. 'You should stay on land if you want to chase girls!'

'Eric's right.' Steve cackled. 'There's only fish down there. And soon the three of us, but I don't think you'd fancy seeing me in a seashell bra. Maybe Eric on a bad day.'

'Hey!' I smacked him.

Dex grimaced. 'I didn't mean *that* kind of mermaid.'

'What other mermaids are out there? The top half's the fish?' Steve joked.

'Nevermind.' Dex averted his gaze, clutching the

sketchbook he brought to kill time with.

I raised an eyebrow. 'Tell us about it on the way down.'

He shook his head. 'You won't get a word out of me once we start breathing helium.'

***

Cramped inside the small metal chamber of the diving bell, already saturated, the only sounds were Dex's pencil scratching against paper and the eerie noises of the descent into the ocean's depths.

'What the cursed fuck is that?!' Steve exclaimed, looking at the page. His helium-high voice made me burst out in laughter. Dex flinched and covered the page with his hand, his splayed fingers shielding the picture beneath.

I snatched the sketchbook from him. The creature on the page was man-shaped, with gills down its neck and gaping between its ribs. Fins traced its limbs, giving the illusion of a mermaid tail. A bridge of sharp teeth lined its mouth like a reef shark's.

'It will give me nightmares.' Steve frowned. 'Sick imagination.'

Dex broke his silence. 'I didn't invent it. I've dived with him.'

Steve crossed his arms. 'What depth?'

'One hundred twenty metres.'

I gave him a hard stare and two words. 'Nitrogen narcosis.'

The way Dex shook his head as the last light faded made me feel uneasy.

'I dived with him *before* he became like this. He inhaled

seawater—'

'Stop fooling around.' I scrunched up the page and tossed it onto the floor. 'The only thing you become breathing water is *dead*.'

***

Dex wasn't intimidated by the colossal squid stretching its pipe-network tentacles across the ocean floor. He manoeuvred well in the water, unfazed by the shadows and faint lights of sea life lurking around the rig before revealing their strange forms. But there was something about the way he would stop moving from time to time. How his eyes would go unfocused. Even if we waved a hand in front of his face or called his name, he wouldn't respond.

I got into the habit of shoving him off the pipes when he spaced out, to snap him out of it. He'd raise a hand, a sign for "I'm okay" and climb back to carry on bolting on the new parts. Already cold to the bones, I didn't need the chilling thought he was looking at something I couldn't see: a *mermaid* emerging from the shadows.

Inside the bell, he kept drawing that one guy.

Insomnia set in by the end of the first week. We laid sleepless on our narrow bunks. Dex ocean-gazed with a hand on the porthole, his eyes lost in the darkness. Unmoving, for hours.

'Aren't they beautiful?' he whispered.

A chill ran down my spine. There was nothing but the black void staring back at us.

I no longer wished to look out the portholes, and on the rig I kept my eyes on the pipes we worked on, on the valves that needed turning. Not on the dark waters, and not on Dex Turner staring deep into them.

***

I woke to a scraping sound. Some metallic rustling. Dex sat by his porthole as usual, fiddling with something around the glass.

'What are you doing...?' I asked.

'He is here.' He turned towards me. I could just make out a screwdriver in his hands. 'I'm letting him in.'

Jumping off my bed, I slammed my fist onto the lightswitch.

Steve sat up in confusion. 'What's happening?'

Not answering my crewmate, I threw Dex onto the floor and twisted the screwdriver from his grasp. He'd gone mad. There was no telling what he would be capable of if he so loved his imaginary mermaids, the ones you create by drowning a diver.

'Tie his hands,' I ordered.

***

When Steve took him outside, I didn't follow. Dex stepped into the exit hole, into the cold water. Barefoot and no helmet. No gas. Taking a deep breath, he plunged under like he was just going for a short walk. Steve followed, grim faced, fully equipped.

On return, Steve removed his helmet, muttering one anchor-weight word, heavy enough to forever pull us down. *Drowned*. No relief came, just shivers. The image of Dex and his mermaid whirlpooled inside my head. Our troubled breathing filled the space for a few minutes, or hours, before the tapping began. All around on the walls. Like a force against the cracks in our sanity. It wouldn't stop. He wouldn't stop. Circling the bell, he passed the portholes, fins trailing as he swam. His lips stretched to an open smile, showcasing a mouthful of sharp teeth.

Whispered Secrets – Anne-Marie Kofoed

(Genre: Drama)

I still remember the first secret whispered into my wooden ear, my paint still fresh and shiny. The girl's pigtails whipped in the early summer wind as my world spun around, the cheery carousel music weaving its tune around us.

"I want to be a ballerina and spin just like you when I grow up." Her small hand smoothed over my neck. "I want a blue leotard, blue like you." A kind pat was my reward when the music stopped.

The same girl returned months later, her feet skipping the newly fallen leaves. Her eyes were bright as she jumped on my back, wrapping her arms around my neck. "I take ballet classes now." Her cheek rubbed against my hard mane as she whispered into my ear, "Mom says I'm a natural."

Every year the girl returned to my world, each time with a new secret to whisper in my ear. She told me stories of ballets and the intricate steps she had to learn, such as pirouettes and arabesque. I wished I could see her dance and twirl around in the pink ballet shoes she told me about. My paint became a little less shiny.

I watched her grow up and looked forward to her next whispered secret. Countless young boys and girls rode on my back each year, but only she whispered stories to me.

One year she didn't show up. I worried as I spun around in my locked position. It was a sad year, made worse when a wild boy set his teeth into my ear, gnawing a chip off my wood.

One year became two. When I saw the girl she'd changed, her face less round, almost grown up, her hair in a short style. Her approach was slower as she limped to my side, and her sad eyes shifted over my form, a small smile spreading over her lips.

"I missed you," she whispered as she managed to situate herself on my back. Slumped over my neck, she proclaimed, "I won't spin anymore." Her voice caught in her throat. The ride began and her hand kept sliding up and down my neck. She leaned closer to my chipped ear, and her fingers touched the exposed wood. "We're both broken. Can you still hear me?"

The girl never returned. I still spin and make children laugh. It's my life, but I can't help wondering what happened to the girl. There is no shine to my paint any longer.

One day a young woman carrying a small child strides toward me as fast as her limp allows her. "Mary, you must hold on." I hear the familiar lilt in her voice; she's older, but she is my favorite girl.

"Momma, stay, please."

"Okay." She smooths her hand over my neck, caressing my chipped ear. "I've missed you, old friend," she whispers.

When the music stops, the child cries out, "Can we come back again, please, Mom?"

My paint peels off into the mother's hand and I lose all hope. But a smile blooms over her face when she says, "We'll come every year, Pumpkin." She pats my wound, saying, "Our friend here needs us, and next visit, we'll shine his coat and mend his ear."

Wishes Are For Children – Kay Northbridge

(Genre: Drama)

My father clutched his chest as I blew to make my sixteenth wish. The next sun rose before my birthday was remembered – wishes are for children. Marked by my mother with a six-wick orange candle and an oval locket. A picture of my father nestled in the silver.

"Allow yourself tonight to grieve," she said, "but you're a grown-up now. One night will be enough."

Worn every day, an ornament, like the smile on my face, I kissed it on waking and as the sun set. The candle had real slices of orange and delicate blossom enrobed in its sweet-scented wax. I saved it for twelve years. Until the night I got the call.

A sorrowful nurse shook her head as she met me. Tears fell. More saline along the clinical corridors.

I returned home and lit all six wicks. Placing mother's candle by my bed, I rocked myself from side to tearful side. I whispered in the flickering shadows: "Allow yourself tonight to grieve, but you're a grown up now. One night will be enough."

The curtains caught as I drifted into dreams. I awoke to crackling, smoke-heavy air. Pulling myself, lightheaded, from my covers, I staggered towards sirens and blue flashes. Smashing glass, deep voices, then reflective uniforms, showed me my exit.

Something snagged at my neck as my rescuer reached rough hands around me.

A house can be rebuilt. But my locket was lost to the flames. And wishes are for children.

Zephyr's Freedom Selfie – Trevor Woods

(Genre: Drama)

Captain Zephyr pilots the ship atop the decaying Statue of Liberty. The afterburn of the ship's atomic engine sends jungle foliage and dust into the air. Now landed, Zephyr presses a translucent button with foreign symbology.

The captain's door opens—*hissssssss.*

Stepping out, Zephyr examines the ancient ruins of Lady Liberty overlooking now abandoned New York City, once a symbol of freedom. Now, the millennia-old relic reminds sightseers of humanity's downfalls—greed, tribalism, war, and incivility.

"Hi, Earth," Zephyr says while taking a selfie, offering a peace sign. Earth is now a trending backdrop for tourists from distant galaxies.

Author Biographies

Alexis Araneta

Alexis is an author from Manila, Philippines primarily writing drama and romance stories. Passionate about words since childhood, she began writing at the age of nine and has won several writing awards as a student.

When not torturing her protagonists emotionally, she enjoys learning languages, listening to 70s jazz and soul music, and watching musical theatre.

Anna Sharples

Anna is a fiction author, poet and editor. She was a finalist in the 2023 Globe Soup Genre Smash competition and is working on her first novel alongside shorter writing projects. Following a Classics degree from the University of Cambridge, she managed publications for the University's colleges for seven years before founding Sharp-sighted Grammar, a freelance editing business. She posts writing and editing videos on TikTok @anna.sharples.editor

Anne-Marie Kofoed

Anne-Marie lives in Denmark and hides in the magic between the pages of a book whenever real life allows it. With three girls and a loving husband in her life, she navigates through life with her muse as her constant companion.

An avid reader as a child, she soon began to write stories of her own. Though comfortable with the long form, she currently has fallen in love with flash and microfiction, regularly competing in international writing contests.

Instagram: kofoed779new

April Pereira

April Pereira (she/they) is a proud Azorean-American originally from Fall River, MA. From wrangling words as a publisher to fostering more inclusive communities through storytelling, April's career has been as diverse as their taste in sci-fi captains (Pike or Picard? The debate rages on). When not summoning fantastical creatures from the lands of Jaqor (D&D, anyone?), April chills with a good book or knits epic scarves. After conquering both coasts, they now rule a cozy kingdom in the PNW, fueled by books, yarn, and perfectly brewed tea. Find them on social media (@crafty.bookwyrm) or at aprilpereira.com!

Beth Connor

Beth is a weaver of tales, captivated by creating and fueled by a love for storytelling.

Chris Morris

Chris Morris once came 4th in the final round of an NYC Midnight contest, hasn't stopped bragging about it, and will use absolutely any opportunity to bring it up, including in author bios. He is a writer, support for learning assistant, and musician (well, a drummer). He lives in Dundee, Scotland with his young daughter and tries his best for her to maybe one day say: "He's alright, you know."

Cindy Strube

Cindy doesn't like to write third-person biographies. Chickens insist on appearing in many of her stories.

Claire Lindsey

Claire is a music educator who resides in Texas. Her work has won awards in contests such as Writer's Playground, Reedsy, and Globe Soup. When she is not teaching or writing, she enjoys agility training with her dog, Maya.

C.P. Misola

C.P. Misola is a Filipino-British writer. Lover of all short-form stories, from the nano to the novella, she pens her tales whilst nestled in Somerset's Blackdown Hills, with her two cats, Luci and Casper.

She is currently working on her first collection of folk horror short stories that feature tales born from the rich cultural and historical landscape of the Philippines.

Cristina Rose Strube

Just a hobbyist with no real ambition. Would be content to daydream all of the time if that were sustainable.

Daniel R. Hayes

Daniel lives in Brandywine, West Virginia, and is a horror/supernatural author. He has written over 200 short stories, and his first novel, "Tales from Mr. Macabre," was published in 2022.

His second novel, "Hot Head," is set for a 2024 release.

He loves spending time with his beautiful daughter and is an avid bodybuilder. In his spare time, he enjoys destressing by watching films or disappearing into a video game.

David McCahan

Oxygen. Dogs. Whiskey. Sunshine. Second birthday 10/8/10. Original birthday quite a bit earlier.

Deidra Whitt Lovegren

Deidra Whitt Lovegren has written over one hundred short stories and regularly competes in international writing contests.

Her novel The Medicine Girl debuted in July 2022. The sequel The Medicine Woman was released in August 2023. Her shorter works include 21 Conversations, a collection of dialogue-only stories, and The Lady of the Match, a short story collection translated into Arabic that premiered at the Cairo International Book Fair in 2024.

Over her teaching career, Deidra has taught scores of English classes from preschool to college. Currently, she is the upper school director at a private high school.

She lives in Virginia with her husband of 30 years, three sons, and two rescue cats: Cinnamon Girl and Marty.

Del Griffith

Del is a retired math teacher. A firm proponent of good Texas brisket, fine Irish whiskey, and Agatha Christie (when she tries).

Slipping the surly bonds of expectations when he writes. A fan of banned books and grunge music. Trying to appease gravity is his day job.

Eamon Somers

After 37 years facilitating the construction of social housing in the UK, Eamon Somers returned (2023) to his native Ireland. His stories have appeared in Chroma, Tees Valley Writer, and Automatic Pilot, and the anthologies of Breakthrough Books. The Journal of Truth and Consequence (University of Phoenix) nominated his Fear of Landing for a Pushcart Prize. Eamon's debut novel Dolly Considine's Hotel, set in Dublin, was published in 2021. An LGBTQ+ activist, his story Nataí Bocht featured in Quare Fellas published by Basement Press in Ireland, and provided the inspiration for his forthcoming novel, The Man Who Gave It Away.

Hannah P. Simmons

Hannah is a rising author whose love of writing delves into many areas. She has a special interest in fantasy and religious literature, but also enjoys delving into poetry and even film. Her work has been published in the Winner's Circle of Reedsy Prompts, as well as the Blue Marble Storytellers podcast.

Hannah has served as an editor and screen writer for such productions as "The Da Vinci Monologues" for Discovery Place Science in North Carolina, and the YouTube series "Rise of the Phoenix" for Artist Universe.

You can find her latest stories on her YouTube channel, "The Daily Feels", or her Reedsy blog "The Daily Post".

James Lynch

James is a writer of fiction, mostly fantasy and light sci-fi. You can find his prose in We Suck at Comics, Volume 1 – Rejection (available now) and Volume 2 – Coloring Outside the Lines (both produced by Wayward Raven Media), Fall Into Fantasy 2024 (Cloaked Press), and The Book of Choices Volume 1 (Wolf Grove Media).

You can follow James on JamesLynchAuthor.com. When he's not writing or reading (or blogging about those activities), he enjoys cooking, swimming, roller coasters, and attending comic conventions.

He lives in New York with his amazing wife and dynamic son.

J.I. Mumford

Fueled by bouts of insomnia and stolen moments during union-mandated tea breaks, Mumford crafts worlds of wonder and whimsy. By day, he's a special effects engineer at London's Natural History Museum. His home, complete with an apple tree besieged by voracious parakeets, often sparks story ideas. When not writing or tending to Jurassic giants, Mumford practices Kung Fu, seeking balance in both physical and literary forms. This self-taught writer, with a few honorable mentions in short story contests, blends Curio Fiction with Psychological Horror, drawing inspiration from London life and his misadventures in Arkansas.

Jon Casper

Originally from Pasadena, California, Jon currently calls Rochester, New York home, where he lives with his wife, Andrea, and their three cats.

A lifelong fan of Science Fiction, Jon enjoys themes exploring human consciousness and the nature of reality, especially the role technological advancements play in highlighting, or disrupting, these constructs.

He has published two novels: Antisocial and Tantalus Awaits.

Kay Northbridge

Just a horror fan trying to learn the craft of writing. Sometimes the two things converge.

K. L. Vincent

K. L. Vincent's background as an occupational therapist and educator has given her an understanding of human behavior and resilience, further enriched by her own neurodivergence, which she channels into her storytelling. Her literary accomplishments include multiple accolades in Globe Soup's fiction challenges and a forthcoming short story in the Book of Choices by Wolf Grove Media.

Michał Przywara

Michał is a Canadian writer who has written over a hundred short stories, in a variety of genres. His stories often contain humour and absurd elements.

He's a prolific reader, and just as he's been influenced to write by various fantastic authors, he hopes to inspire others to take up the pen as well.

When he's not writing prose by night, he's writing code by day.

Michelle Oliver

Michelle writes in the margins of her own busy life as a mum and teacher. Her short stories have been recognised in various online competitions, and she hopes one day to finish that novel that's gathering dust in the corner of her life.

Míriam Toyama

Míriam is Brazilian, graduated in Economics, has a PhD, and is a teacher. She has a published short story on the Anthology Book of Choices and is a writer for Pletora of Pop and Waxing Lyrical on Medium.

Misty Mator

Misty Mator is a professional Narrative Performer with a degree in Written & Performative Storytelling. She has performed for venues like the Women's Storytelling Festival in Washington D.C., Six Feet Apart Productions, and Pittsburgh's Children's Theatre Festival and has conducted workshops for groups like Story Crossroads and Carnegie Mellon University.

In 2022, she learned about NYC Midnight and entered on a whim, unaware this would ignite an addiction to writing contests with riddling parameters. Camaraderie with an amazing international community of writers, often working under crazy contest deadlines, is one of her life's unexpected joys.

Connect with her at www.storytellermistymator.com

Riel Rosehill

Riel Rosehill is a fiction writer focusing on speculative, character-focused stories.

She won the November 2022 Secret Attic Short Story Contest, was shortlisted on Reedsy and received an honorable mention on Writers Playground in the Sixth Playground Challenge. Her work has appeared in The Ulu Review and on The NoSleep podcast among other podcasts and anthologies.

Currently, she is working on her first novel.

Riel grew up in Budapest and now lives in the UK.

Robert Burns

Robert Burns is a classically trained architect who brings a designer's eye to his fiction.

A writer in a number of different genres, his stories have appeared in numerous online publications as well as several print anthologies, including a fantasy story focusing on Novel Characters, a piece of detective fiction, a dystopian Christmas tale, and the first chapter of a historic novel currently in the works.

OH! And he loves the micros.

Robert writes full time from his home in Richmond, Virginia.

Russell Mickler

Russell writes fantasy and science fiction. His micro and flash work appears in several short story anthologies and magazines. Black Anvil Books is Mickler's imprint for self-published fantasy and serialized fiction.

www.black-anvil-books.com

Suma Jayachandar

Suma Jayachandar, a teacher, lives with her family in India. A wanderer, she writes to make sense of humanity shaped by seemingly random acts of kindness and cruelty.

When no answers show up, she finds peace in pruning the houseplants and feeding the stray cats.

thomas iannucci

thomas iannucci is a writer, poet, and rapper from Kaua'i, Hawaii. His work has been published in literary journals like Bamboo Ridge, New Zealand's Takahē Magazine, and The Hawaii Review of Books, amongst others. In his writing, as in all of his art, he seeks to explore the human experience, particularly when peeling back the harmful perception of "paradise" that so deeply affects Hawaii. You can find him on social media @thomasiannucci for the latest updates on his work.

Thom Brodkin

Thom Brodkin's short stories have circled the globe. From being featured in a Swedish textbook to a Moroccan anthology to a Japanese Zine, readers worldwide enjoy his relatable characters and transcendent themes that warm the soul. One of his recent works has been adapted to the screen and featured in several international film competitions. He resides in Central Virginia with his family and beloved miniature schnauzers, Salt and Milo.

Trevor Woods

Trevor crafts stories of speculative fiction and drama. When he's not creating post-apocalyptic and sci-fi worlds or discovering new fears to unlock, he's helping institutionalized veterans transition from service by guiding them through career exploration and self-reflection.

Outside of his writing endeavors, he plays fetch with his Golden Retriever, Maggie, and spends quality time with his family of six, exploring the vibrant culture of the Windy City.

Victor D. Sandiego

Victor D. Sandiego lives in the high desert of central Mexico.

His work appears in various journals and has been featured on public radio. He is the founder of Subprimal Poetry Art and the founder/editor of Dog Throat Journal, an online publication of short fiction and prose poetry.

More of his work can be found on Dynamic Creed, where he publishes evocative creative fiction for those who enjoy thoughtful, edgy stories that provoke reflection upon our shared human condition.

www.bluemarblestorytellers.com

www.ingramcontent.com/pod-product-compliance
Lightning Source LLC
Chambersburg PA
CBHW060428310726
48977CB00001B/93